Some
Merry-Go-Round
Music

Some Merry-Go-Round Music

by MARY STOLZ

Harper & Brothers
Publishers, New York

Library of Congress catalog card number: 59–5323

To Janet, the two Burnleys, and Ned

Some
Merry-Go-Round
Music

Chapter One

PUMFRET & SON, Knit Goods, was a small firm in a huge, dark building near Wall Street. All day, now that it was summer, embattled traffic sent its roar through open windows, and in Miranda Parrish's corner of the outer office a dusty fan on top of the filing cabinets turned its big head from side to side and wheezed and stirred the heavy air like batter in a bowl. The air was sticky, the typewriter balky, the two salesmen peevish. They had gotten their schedules confused and had arrived at what was termed the Home Office at the same time, which meant that one of them had to sit in a chair in the display room while the other used the desk. Even when the two Mr. Pumfrets, junior and senior, were out, neither of the salesmen used their desks.

Probably because I'm here, Miranda thought. They think I'll tell on them, which is very unperceptive. I never talk to Mr. Pumfret at all if I can help it, and John Jr. couldn't defend a pencil, much less something as big as a desk.

Naturally, Mr. Wyeland got the desk in the display room. He'd called Miranda in, dictated at some length, then leaned back and waited for his letters to be ready to sign. Mr. Camp, in the display room, fidgeted, frowned, and held his peace.

This office, thought Miranda, typing a series of dull letters on the fall line of men's hose, consists of three cowards and two bullies. We should hire another bully to make it even. And then she thought, oh well, I won't be here long.

She often said this to herself, without ever defining how long was long. In business school she'd dreamed of a beautiful office on Madison or Park Avenue. An office with air conditioning and rugs and shining walls of windows. She'd never much thought what the actual job would be, but the office had been a dream place. She'd almost gotten a job that was almost what she wanted in a brokerage firm that had a huge airy stenographers' room and a lounge for coffee breaks. But they'd given the place to someone else, and Miranda, in a panic for fear she'd get no job at all, took this when it was offered to her, and had been here for a year telling herself it wouldn't be long.

Later, when Mr. Wyeland had left, Mr. Camp came to her in a hesitant manner that inclined her to listen more pleasantly than the heat and the hour and the end of the week's work would indicate. With a grimace on his little face, he said, "Honestly, Miranda, I don't know what to do. Here're these letters I wanted to get out, and then that fellow loads you down, to say nothing of I guess you have plenty of the Pumfrets' stuff to do, huh?"

"Well, I do," she said, but not forbiddingly. She'd nearly finished. What was left of Mr. Pumfret's work could, in a pinch, wait till Monday.

"I'd do it myself, sort of," he explained. "Only I can't type for beans . . ."

"All right," Miranda said, knowing Mr. Camp could spend twenty minutes telling you how he had to leave in five. "Let's get at them, shall we?"

Mr. Camp looked happy. "This is darned nice of you, Miranda. Darned nice. I'll bet there aren't many girls in many offices who'd do a thing like this. Last place I had a desk, do you know what the girl did? Got mad at me one day for dictating too much, *she* thought—it was just my regular work and no more than anybody else'd have, but that's what she thought—and she began to make these great scrawly huge shorthand figures that even I could tell were angry, so I cut it short but just the same she came back to me in about half an hour and said now look what I'd made her do, she couldn't read a thing and I'd have to do the letters all over again. As if it was *my* fault."

Miranda looked commiserating, but she knew a touch of envious sympathy for the unknown girl. Imagine telling a man he'd have to do his dictation over. She considered Mr. Pumfret's face if she . . . but the fancy wouldn't even go into words. "I'm ready if you are, Mr. Camp," she said, gently guiding.

3

"Why don't you call me Charlie?" he asked in a plaintive tone. "Over and over I ask you to call me Charlie. . . ."

She'd never asked him to call her Miranda, but didn't know how to ask him not to. "I couldn't, Mr. Camp. Not in the office."

His eyes lit, and she groaned inwardly. Now, why had she said that? "Mr. Camp," she said quickly, "please don't ask me again. I can't go out with you, honestly."

"But why not?" he said, meekly persistent. "I just don't see why not. Plenty of fellows take out girls from their offices. It's not like Mr. Pumfret would object or anything. Anyway, who's he to say who you can go out with? He's not your father."

"He certainly isn't. And he hasn't said I can't go out with you. He'd die of shock if I went asking him for permission to go on dates. So let's just drop it, please, Mr. Camp."

"But I don't see why—" he began again.

Suppose I said, "Mr. Camp, I won't go out with you because I'm five foot seven and you're five foot three." Suppose I said, "Mr. Camp, to me you look like a radiator cap, even when I'm sitting down." She never made personal remarks aloud, but she thought them, and sometimes, with Mr. Camp, was tempted to speak them. He was so maddeningly timorous and determined.

It isn't fair, she thought irritably, her temper demoralized by stale hot air, by too much work, by boredom. It just isn't *fair* for a man to look so shy and be so . . . so *gnat*like. Go away and leave me alone, she growled in her mind, and allowed a scowl to crease her forehead. She had found that with Mr. Camp a frown was more efficacious than kindly explanations that weren't true.

He began dictating, handing out his words at such a thoughtful pace that Miranda all but screamed, "Mr. Camp, nobody can take dictation this slowly. I'd take it faster than this if I didn't know how to take it at all." But she said nothing. She plodded along a few words ahead of him and wondered why it was that short men always took to tall girls. It had been the same in high school. The boys who came up to her nose just adored her, and the six-footers all wanted little bitty girls in flats. *Men,* said Miranda to herself, feeling original and justified.

Finally Mr. Camp ground to a halt. "Is it too much for you, Miranda?" he asked anxiously. "I don't want to impose on you."

"Not at all," she said briskly, making an elaborate business of setting her notebook in position, so that at least he'd remember it was late and wouldn't impose further. Actually, she did not mind doing his letters, poor man. She just minded him.

"You won't change your mind—" he began, and for once Miranda was glad to have Mr. Pumfret's buzzer sound.

It developed that Mr. Pumfret had all kinds of second thoughts about a four-page letter she'd finished earlier that afternoon.

"Sorry to have to ask you to do this so late," he said, not sounding sorry. "Maybe you can save that middle page. Not touched, you see. Space your words, or whatever you do."

Rigid with indignation, Miranda swallowed, dropped her eyes to hide their fury, and said, "That's all right, Mr. Pumfret." It's only the end of the day and the end of the week and the hottest day and week of the summer so far. That's perfectly all right, Mr. Pumfret, you pill. She started away, almost trembling.

"Oh, Miss Parrish?"

"Yes, sir?" She turned slowly to face him.

"Finish it up tonight. I'll sign it first thing Monday morning. Have to get it out early Monday."

"Yes, Mr. Pumfret," she said shakily.

A man only slightly more sensitive than the president of Pumfret & Son would have guessed that something was amiss somewhere, but Mr. Pumfret merely nodded and reached for his straw hat. "See you Monday," he said, going out through her small anteroom. "Be sure to lock up." Mr. Camp said good night, and flushed when the door closed on no reply.

"Absent-minded character," he said, blustering a little.

Miranda, rarely too annoyed to help save someone's face (she considered embarrassment catching, like a disease), said, "He's often like that. Just don't pay any attention." Feeling that was sufficient, she sat at her typewriter and began banging away so fiercely that Mr. Camp, who *was* more sensitive than the president of Pumfret & Son, rubbed his perspiring upper lip and left with a good night so low she could have ignored it.

"Good night," she said at the last minute, and when the door had closed behind him debated whether to burst into tears.

Dear little Mr. Camp could say all he wanted to about not imposing, once having made sure she had the letters. He hadn't said a word about imposition when she came out of Mr. Pumfret's office, had he? Certainly not. What if she'd said, "Well, I do have an awful lot to do and now that old pig has given me more, so could your letters wait maybe till next week?" No, Mr. Camp hadn't taken any chances on that, had he?

Suddenly she stood, pushed the typewriter into its well, turned off the lights and left the office. She jiggled the knob, to make sure the door was locked, and walked to the elevator as if planning a hold-up.

"What's eating you?" said Connie Marks, coming along at the same moment. She worked in an office down the hall, and the two of them sometimes had lunch together. "Heat got you?" she asked. She looked trim and unaffected by the weather, and was conscious of it. She had an unendearing way of saying she just loved the heat and didn't see why people complained so.

To forestall hearing it again, Miranda said, "No. I dote on the heat." Connie looked pointedly at her crumpled dress, the damp tendrils of hair curling at brow and neck. I forgot to put on lipstick, Miranda thought. Darn. "Dote on it," she repeated. "I'm just tired of working."

"Who isn't? Still—" They got in the elevator. It

7

smelled of armpits "—still and all, it's Friday. Another day, another devalued dollar, and a weekend coming up. Got any interesting dates?"

"No."

Connie shook her head. They walked out on the baking sidewalk, littered and thronged. "That steady of yours away again?"

"Yes," said Miranda uncomfortably.

"Honestly, honey, don't you think you're carrying this faithful stuff too far? I mean, hanging around this way waiting for a guy who's practically always somewhere else is madness. I mean, really, where's the harm in you going out once in a while? Do you suppose he's sitting around reading *Boys' Life* all the time? Where's he this time?"

"Buffalo," said Miranda, because it was the only city she could think of. Mr. Pumfret had addressed three letters there today.

"This fella that I told you about," said Connie. "This floorwalker at Macy's, you know, he'd still like to meet you. He was with I and Joe the other night and we started talking about you, and he said are you anything like me, and I said gosh no, she's just the opposite—" Connie preened a little "—so he said in that case bring her on. He's a howl. You'd like him. Got a real sense of humor. So just don't tell your steady, that's all. He don't have to know everything. None of them have to."

More and more uneasy, Miranda shook her head. "It's just that I . . . well, I just don't feel like seeing someone else, Connie. It's just a feeling I have."

"Honestly, I don't understand you," said Connie. But she looked vaguely respectful of such constancy. "Well, here's my bus. So long, honey. If you change your mind, gimme a ring, yeah?"

"I will," said Miranda. She watched Connie mount the bus steps, saw the quick interested glances that her long curving legs won from passing men.

She's right in one way, Miranda thought. I'm her opposite. She thought about this as she descended to the subway and moved in the ignominious press of sweating, weary, absent-eyed, latently hostile homebound workers. Managing to wriggle (or be thrust) into an uptown express, she leaned against the doors as they slammed shut, tried to breathe shallowly of the unpleasant air, and considered what she looked like.

Plain, if you weren't in a word-mincing mood, and she wasn't. A teacher had once told her she looked demure, and Mr. Camp had once called her refreshing. Well, no doubt a plain girl could be both of these. Soft brown hair with a tendency to curl, smooth olive complexion, brown eyes, tall, too slim. Not skinny. But no Connie, nor ever likely to be.

This steady of hers, the one that she'd used first to discourage Mr. Camp and then to prevent Connie from inveigling her into dates with people who sounded horrible, was getting to be an . . . an albatross, she decided, remembering a poem she'd studied and disliked in her last year of high school. Except, remembering further, that wasn't a good example because the albatross was

9

around the poor fellow's neck for ages, and her steady was not only not around her neck, he wasn't around anybody's because he didn't exist.

I don't only not have a steady, I don't even have a once-in-a-while. How *did* girls meet people? Nice people, that was. Some of the girls she knew still saw boys they'd gone with in school, but Miranda, though she'd had dates, hadn't inspired anyone with the will to pursue her beyond the portals of the George Washington High School. In business school she'd been too busy working even to worry about dates. But now . . .

I'm nineteen. I've never been in love, and no one has been in love with me.

"Troubles, girlie?"

Inadvertently, Miranda glanced at the speaker. A sharp-featured sharply dressed young man returned her look with bold glassy eyes. His lips curved with confidence and self-satisfaction. Miranda looked away hastily, tried to see if there were somewhere else she could move to, though she knew there was not, and stuck her nose in the air.

"That's right," he murmured. "I like 'em snooty." He moved closer, and Miranda squeezed herself as small as she could, feeling ill. "C'mon, c'mon," he said. "Where're you goin' with that big sigh, sounded like you was dyin' for sumthin'. I could bring you back to life, believe me, I could—"

Miranda, pressing her lips together, turned her head away.

"C'mon," he was murmuring moistly, "c'mon and tell ,what I can do for you, and, believe me, I could do plenty for you, I could—"

Miranda turned and faced him suddenly. "You can call a policeman, that's what you can do," she said in a loud shaky voice. She tried to glare into his shallow eyes, but could not meet them at all.

"Ah . . . for—" He shoved through a wall of people, away from her, indifferent to the irritation he aroused, and Miranda stood, trembling a little, her eyes down in case anyone was looking, for the remainder of the interminable ride. She didn't think about him. She didn't think about herself, or about love. She thought of nothing as she waited for her station, when she'd be set free of the subway.

Chapter Two

THE PARRISHES lived in Washington Heights, in an old building with a gritty courtyard, a lobby floored with little octagonal tiles that always showed the grey streaky marks of the janitor's mop, and apartments that were painted every three years but somehow always looked as if the three years were about up. Fire escapes climbed the yellow brick façade and now in midsummer were alive with people and plants and mops and pets. Women in folding chairs sat close to the buildings, flopping cardboard fans close to their faces, talking languidly. Here and there a dog sprawled on his side, panting tongue dripping on the sidewalk. Men in shirt sleeves leaned against lamp posts, leaned out of the windows, walked along slowly, fanning themselves with straw hats.

Miranda turned into her building, ignored the old-fashioned grille elevator, climbed two flights to her apartment, found the door unlocked and entered.

She heard her brother, Barney, in the living room at

the end of the long hall, blowing softly on his clarinet. Miranda glanced into the empty kitchen, dark now as it was dark at any time of the day, and saw that nothing had been started for dinner.

She walked down the hall. "Mama not home yet?" she said to Barney.

He lowered his clarinet, looked up and shook his head. "Nope."

"You left the door unlocked again."

"Miranda, you fracture me, you really do. Are burglars going to find this neighborhood irresistible? Tell me, what's a burglar going to *find* here?" He glanced down at the instrument in his hand. "Except this, of course. This is valuable."

"Well, then."

"Maybe I'll remember."

Miranda sat down, pushing off her shoes. "What a day. And I have to go back tomorrow."

"Saturday?" said Barney. "Listen, Miranda, you don't have to work on Saturday, no matter what old Pumpy says, you hear me? You getting overtime?"

"No. I just didn't finish today."

"Finish Monday," he said grimly. "I mean it. Don't go in there and work on Saturday without overtime. Even overtime isn't worth it, in this heat."

"It can't be helped," she said, wishing she hadn't mentioned it. Barney was strongly pro-union, and never seemed to understand that in an office the size of Pumfret's there was no union, and no union hours. And it could have been helped. She could have done Mr. Pumfret's letter and simply let Mr. Camp's work wait until she got to it. Only she couldn't bear the thought of his poor little face on Monday if she told him his letters weren't ready. Probably people were always putting him off.

"Do you know why it can't be helped?" Barney said, leaning forward and fixing her with stern eyes. "You know why? Because you're an exploitable type, that's why. You have a face that lights up and says Patsy. Miranda, are you ever going to get any character?"

"I guess not," she said sadly. Barney was always lecturing her, as if he were three years older than she was, instead of the other way around.

"And you don't ·even care, that's what gets me." He blew a few notes on his clarinet, put it down again and scowled at her. "You don't give a darn that anyone at all can take advantage of you."

"It keeps the peace."

"I've been telling you for years that whoever first said peace at any price was some poor slob who was scared of his own shadow and never got it at any price. I tell you, a philosophy like that is a *guarantee* that you're never going to have peace. Do you have peace?"

"No. But I bet you don't either."

"I'm not looking for it," he said. Miranda found this an unsatisfactory answer, but couldn't figure out why.

"Barney, I hear enough wrangling at home here. I will not get involved in it outside."

"That again. After all these years, can't you just close your ears when Pop and Mama start after each other? That's what I do. The minute they begin, I go deaf."

"You can't be deaf to everything."

"I can. If I don't want to hear it, I don't hear it, period."

"That's character?" she asked. "You're always talking about facing everything, but I notice you don't face a thing you don't want to. I notice that when you wanted to stop going with Penny, you didn't face her. I didn't see you going over to her house and saying, 'This is how it is, Penny.' I didn't notice you facing up to that. You just ducked. You had Mama answer the phone and you let the poor girl figure it out for herself. And why, Barney dear? Because it would have disturbed your peace to face her."

"I never said you had to face *all* the challenges in life. You have to meet the important ones. Things where principle and character are involved. You have to be strong enough to see that people don't take advantage of you. The way you can't say no to a salesman at the door— that's weakness, not kindness. Why do we have three brooms, I ask you? Because the guys who sell brooms always seem to get here when *you're* on deck. Why does the—"

"Maybe Penny thought it was important," she interrupted. "And sometimes I don't think you and I agree about what character is. It's all right not to let people take advantage of you, but what about not taking advantage of them? I think it was taking advantage of Penny not to be honest with her, that's what I think."

Barney looked slightly embarrassed. "She wasn't so crazy about me," he mumbled.

Since they both knew he was avoiding the issue, and that he would continue to do so, Miranda let it drop. She leaned back in her chair, half listening as he flirted with the air of "Blue Room."

Barney was a good clarinetist. He was a good thinker, a good person. Intractable, stubborn, awesomely sure of himself, he could be very companionable, and very kind. That is, Miranda thought lazily, he can when it doesn't get in his all-important sixteen-year-old way. Still, most boys—and girls, for that matter—of sixteen were pretty insulated in their own self-importance. Barney was no worse than others. Probably he was some better. Would most boys his age care about their sisters' exploitable characters?

And what sort of life am I going to make with this character? Why, I'm going to work for Pumfret & Son, and once in a while work overtime without getting overtime. I'm going to say no, very sweetly, to invitations from Mr. Camp, and get invited on blind dates with cards that Connie knows. I'm going to encounter creatures like that one on the subway (only that could happen to any girl) and feel sick and then forget them.

She stood up.

"What are you going to do?" Barney asked.

"Get dinner, that's what I'm going to do."

"Bravo. You don't have to sound so fierce about it. Want me to help?"

She smiled. "No, thanks." Barney played a few bars of "The Saints Come Marchin' In." "When do you suppose Mama will be in? Did she say what she planned for dinner?" Miranda asked.

"Are our dinners planned? I thought we just opened the closet door and ate whatever fell out."

"Barney—"

"No, she didn't say what she planned, and she didn't say when she'd be back. She's probably in some neighbor's house and hasn't got the energy to stop talking."

"Barney, you're disrespectful."

"No, I'm not," he said easily. "I just face facts, is all. Not my fault if the fact is Mama's lazy and Pop's simple. I like them anyway."

"Oh, you're so smart." She snatched up her shoes and went down the hall in her stocking feet to her own room. While she changed into a housedress, she heard Barney playing *"Vesti la giubba,"* from *Pagliacci*. He played it almost as if he were laughing. *"Vesti la giubba,"* Barney had told her, meant "Let the Play Go On." "In this case, a comedy," he'd added.

"Is *Pagliacci* a comedy?" she'd asked, surprised.

"Yes, it's a comedy. It's funny the way life is funny, see?"

Miranda, starting dinner, thought now that she certainly did see. She listened to the sad, beautiful air, and thought about her day, and then about Barney. I guess, she decided, he's learned earlier than I have just when it is you're supposed to laugh.

When she got up the following morning, Barney was gone, and her father, who worked nights, hadn't come in yet. Barney had a summer job as a stockboy in a department store. His day off was Monday, and unless it was raining he usually went to Jones Beach and saw to his tan, which was important to him. He was brown and tall and handsome. Miranda was pretty sure that Penny had cared for him deeply. But there was nothing to do about boys or men who grew tired of you, and nothing to do about their ways of showing it. They're all alike, thought Miranda. She had to admit that she based her opinion on magazines, movies and observation, since she'd never been involved enough with a boy or a man to get hurt.

But that's perfectly terrible, she thought, sitting at the kitchen table with a cup of coffee and a sweet bun. Nineteen years old, and not a thing to show for it. No love, no pain, no anything. And maybe I'll get older and older and older and *never* have anything to show for it. I'll become a sere old lady in musty old Pumfret & Son (only by then John Jr. will be Pumfret and *his* boy will be the son) and I'll still have the same balky typewriter and the same listless electric fan, and once in a while I'll remember Connie, who'll have had three husbands by then, and maybe I'll wish I'd met the floorwalker from Macy's. . . .

Because she was young and couldn't really imagine a

future so cheerless, these extravagances put her in a lighter mood. She'd go down to the office and get through those letters in no time. Then there wouldn't be that sense of urgency and pressure she hated so on Monday. Anyway, in two weeks she went on vacation. Who minded a little extra work when no work at all was bobbing along toward you like a bright cork on a wave?

She let herself out of the apartment quietly, because her mother was asleep, and took an almost empty subway down to Chambers Street.

She had finished Mr. Pumfret's revised letter (finding, as she'd known she would, no way to salvage the intact page) and had almost completed Mr. Camp's fussy letters when the door opened and John R. Pumfret, Jr., walked in.

"Hullo," he said, stopping short. "What are you doing here?"

"Working," said Miranda, nervous as if she'd had to say, "Stealing."

"So I see. Why?"

"I didn't finish yesterday. At least, I could have stayed late and finished, but it was hot and I was tired." It irritated her that she sounded defensive.

"I see."

There was a silence, during which each waited for the other to speak.

"Well," said John Jr., looking over her head, "as a matter of fact, I came in to do some work myself. Some letters, that is." Private letters? Miranda wondered. "I saw," he went on, "that you were going to be swamped. With those two idiots coming in at the same time—" he said idiots casually, as if there could be no question of what category the salesmen were in "—so I just thought I'd write off the couple of things I wanted without bothering you."

Miranda was almost literally speechless, and her stare seemed to trouble him. He bobbed his head and went into his father's office. She heard him turn on the fan and sink into the creaky swivel chair.

Well, for heaven's sake, she thought. I wonder if he does this often. He ought, by all she'd heard, to be up in Westchester, sailing his boat. Coming in to do letters in order to save her work? It was incomprehensible.

She glanced at her notebook, slowly resumed typing, stopped again and eyed the wall in front of her, a frown on her forehead. In a moment the frown began to smooth out. Young John, no matter how he tried to make it appear, was not here to save a stenographer work. He was here to catch up on his own work, the same as she was. His father and the brassy salesman had used up all her time until late afternoon, by which time John Jr. had left for a business appointment. Miranda was coolly aware that while John Jr. might attempt to elbow Mr. Camp out of the way (he'd succeed, too, poor Mr. Camp being even more uncertain of his rights than young Mr. Pumfret was), he'd never consider interrupting his father or Mr. Wyeland. That Mr. Pumfret Sr.'s claims came first in the office was unquestioned, and Mr. Wyeland was not a man to let his due be frustrated. So John Jr. had sneaked down to the office today to mend his fences unobserved, and then, when he found he was observed, couldn't resist a chance to make self-interest look like generosity.

Oh, well, thought Miranda, probably most people couldn't. I'm sure I've done it. It was a bit annoying to be put in an apparent position of being obliged to him —after all, she did her work conscientiously, which no one could say of John Jr.—but as long as she'd straightened it out for herself, she didn't care so much. Like many over-accommodating people, Miranda was made uneasy when the situation seemed to be reversed.

She finished Mr. Camp's letters, stacked them neatly aside, got up and knocked at the door of Mr. Pumfret's office.

"Come in," said John Jr. The chair squeaked loudly as he swung about.

He was looking out the window, Miranda thought. Only, why put on this act for me? I have nothing to do with it if he sits and stares at pigeons the whole day. She felt a stir of pity for him. Did he think he had no rights at all, before anyone?

"I could take any letters you want to do, Mr. Pumfret," she said. "If you don't mind if I wait to type them till Monday."

"Not at all," he said graciously.

As if *he* were obliging *me*, Miranda thought, regretting her offer. Barney's right. I have no character, and I'm doing just what I accused John Jr. here of doing. Trying to appear generous. I didn't really want to stay and take his dictation. I want to go home and phone Jenny or Marian or somebody and maybe go to the beach, or anyway plan something for myself for the rest of the day. But here's this lovely chance to seem gracious, and even if I don't feel gracious, I seize it. It's things like this that make it hard for a person to keep her self-respect.

Controlling a rising irritability, she sat, notebook on her knee, waiting. John Jr. took, as always, some frowning minutes to decide what he wanted to say, but once started went along fairly well, if you discounted his jerky delivery.

"Well," he said, some thirty minutes later, "that should do it. At least, that's going to have to do it. I'm tired of the whole thing. I wouldn't care if every man in the country went without socks and underwear for the rest of his life. *Knit goods.* What a way to earn a living."

Miranda looked at him in astonishment as he leaned back, hands clasped behind his neck, and exhaled loudly. He studied her from under drooping lids.

"What are you going to do now?" he asked unexpectedly.

"Do? Well . . . go home, I guess, Mr. Pumfret." What was this about?

"Do you care anything about armor?"

"Armor? You mean like the knights wore?"

"The very same," he drawled.

You pompous prig, Miranda thought. What are you talking to me like that for? The entire Pumfret family had that air of the gentry addressing hoi polloi. Miranda knew they had a nice, modest home in Westchester, and a nice, modest income from the knit-goods business. You'd think they were Vanderbilts, she thought crossly.

"Well, do you?" he persisted, still lounging in his chair, while she stood.

"I don't know anything about it."

"Want to go up to the museum with me and look at some?"

Miranda was dumfounded. John R. Pumfret, Jr., inviting his father's stenographer to go out with him? She supposed she was flattered. After all . . . the boss's son. Connie had never been invited out by her boss's son. Only what, she wondered, is he asking me for? And, furthermore, why am I going to say yes? Just because he *is* the boss's son?

But she knew this was not the entire answer. She was slightly flattered, completely surprised, and somewhat at a loss. No doubt the possibility of being able to say, to Jennie, for instance, "I went out with John R. Pumfret, Jr., the other day," was rather fetching. Perhaps she didn't know how to refuse the boss's son. Which would make me, she reminded herself sternly, sort of a snob, too. I can refuse Mr. Camp and the floorwalker, can't I?

But she knew why she was actually going to agree. It was because, for all his pompous airs, this young man had always seemed sort of sad to her. Sad, uncertain, afraid of his father. She just didn't like the idea of saying

23

no to him. And she was afraid of his father, too. She knew what it felt like.

"How does that strike you as a way to spend a couple of Saturday hours?" he inquired, as if indifferent to how it struck her.

"It might be nice," she said slowly. He was making sure she didn't consider herself booked for the whole day. He really isn't very nice, she thought, and went right on feeling sorry for him. "I've never seen any."

"Let's go," he said, getting to his feet.

Three hours and a hundred scimitars, shields and suits of armor later, they stood before a mounted knight in the Equestrian Court.

"Now," said John R. Pumfret, Jr., "what do you think of this? Magnificent, don't you think?"

"Yes," said Miranda faintly. "If you do." At his expression, she added, "It's *very* magnificent. The greaves, especially." She looked at the plumes on the horsebacked, armored, helmeted figure before her.

"You're looking at the panache. Those are the greaves." He pointed to the legs below the knees of the elegant-looking rider.

Miranda tried to picture the man who had once ridden to battle in these very trappings. He had not been a very big fellow, but he'd carried a weight of steel that a big fellow these days would probably end up on the floor with, clanking helplessly, like a bug on its back. She decided the only man she knew who would fit in these suits of armor was Mr. Camp. Maybe if he had one, she

24

thought, he wouldn't be so afraid of Mr. Pumfret and Mr. Wyeland.

"People have grown a lot, haven't they?" she said. Young Mr. Pumfret was preoccupied and didn't reply. "How did he get on the horse?"

"Hoists, sometimes."

"I suppose," she mused, "that for getting off he had a good chance of being toppled, didn't he? Poor knight."

"There's something else I want to show you," he said. He wanted her to be interested, but scarcely listened to a thing she said. Now he put his hand lightly on her elbow, to indicate they were to move on.

Miranda, as if by accident, turned away, pretending to take a last look around. It removed her elbow from his touch. She went with him obediently to see jeweled scimitars and scabbards and swords in another room. White jade hilts inlaid with gold, with ruby and emerald flowers, with twisting vine patterns. Gem-encrusted foliated scabbards. Even the descriptive words were proud and of another time.

She really rather liked all these things, and if she wasn't completely enjoying the afternoon, that might not be her fault or John R. Pumfret, Jr.'s. It could simply be, she thought, looking at a flowing spiral blade of watered steel, that it's hard to love beauty when you're hungry and your feet hurt.

"Look over here," he said, leading her to another case. "Don't you wish you owned one of those?"

What I really wish, Miranda thought, is that you'd

stop grabbing and nudging every time you want to say something. In the office, when he dictated, or stopped at her desk to leave instructions, he managed without touching her. Practically without looking at her. Of course, in the office she could have told him off. Nicely, but off. What was she to do in this tour of the museum? She'd been practicing, in her mind, saying, "Mr. Pumfret, can't you talk about arms without grabbing mine?" But it wasn't a thing she'd actually say. He wasn't forward, either. She decided it was absent-mindedness and best ignored. "I'd like to own them all," she said, and he looked gratified.

At last he looked at his watch and said, "I'm hungry. I believe I'll have something to eat. How about you?" he added belatedly.

Well, it *is* lunchtime, she informed him in silent vexation. Maybe coats of mail can make you forget lunch, but they can't me. "I'd like something," she admitted, her mouth watering. She'd have liked a whole dinner.

They went to a restaurant where fountains splashed in a pool, and sat at a table beside it, eating sandwiches and iced coffee. *"Au bord du lac,"* said Mr. Pumfret, Jr. He often used French phrases, and Miranda wasn't sure it was polite of him. Of course, maybe he assumed people understood. But, in English or French, they had little to say to each other. She'd finished her sandwich before he spoke again.

"I think the Renaissance armor the most beautiful," he informed her. "How about you?"

In Miranda's mind the various periods were as one. "It's lovely," she said. "All of it."

"Well . . . the medieval," he mused. "Fascinating, but frustrating, wouldn't you say?"

"Why?"

"A complete suit of medieval armor is practically unknown." He frowned heavily at the loss.

"They all looked sort of complete to me."

"Restored," he said glumly.

After a long silence Miranda said, "That was an awfully good sandwich." She was hoping he'd offer her another one. Or some dessert.

He stared at the splashing fountains. "I guess I'd better be getting on up home. Can I take you someplace?" he added, with an honest lack of enthusiasm.

They'd driven from the office to the museum in his sky-blue Ford convertible, and Miranda thought she'd never seen anything so elegant in her life. To be dropped at her apartment door in that would be bliss. She said hesitantly, "I live sort of out of the way," and then remembered that Washington Heights was not out of the way for a person driving to Scarsdale. As she wondered whether she dared amend her answer, he said, "Well, surely I can drop you at a subway?"

"That would be very nice," Miranda sighed.

Chapter Three

HER FATHER was in the living room in his undershirt, a bottle of beer beside him and a ball game blaring. He turned the radio down slightly when she came in.

"Hiya, honeybunch. Whére you been?"

"I went down to the office for a—"

"On Satidday?" he interrupted. "What're they runnin' down there, a sweatshop?"

"Oh, Pop. I've been through it all with Barney. I went in because I wanted to. You work twelve hours a day and I don't wave union hours at you."

"I do it because I gotta," he said. "A hackie's different to other people. You work on the basis a hackie works, you gotta work my hours or the family starves. But *you* don't have to work on no Satidday."

"Today I did."

"You're just too nice for your own good. You're the sweetest, most obligin' little girl in the world, that's what you are."

Miranda, who knew she was nothing of the kind, looked gently at her father, who would never alter his opinion on this subject. Or on any other, for that matter. "I'm glad to see you resting, for a change," she said. "Is that the Yankees you're listening to?"

"Naw. This is the Pirates and Cards." He sounded despondent. Since the Giants had left town, he'd been like a lost, questing soul. "I'da even gone for the Brooks," he explained frequently, but aggrievedly. "Only not them Yankees." Now he shrugged and said, "I just about made up my mind. I guess it's the Cards for me."

"But they're in last place, aren't they?"

"Sixth," he corrected sternly. "Anyways, where was the Giants all the past four-five years? And I never waved in my loyalty, did I?"

Miranda smiled. "Well, but look where they are now. Why don't you keep going for them, now that they're at the top?"

"Judases," he said. "Sold theirselves for pieces of gold."

"Oh, now, Pop. That's not true."

"It's my opinion, Miranda, and I'm stuck with it. I mighta stood the Brooks. . . . Had a fare today, said he flew in from Indianapolis the other day. They flew over Ebbets Field. Looked peaceful and green as a graveyard, he said. I'd hate to fly over the Polo Grounds, I told him. Not that I ever get to fly anywheres, but just the same . . . " He swallowed some beer, wiped his mouth. "You been down that office a heck of a long time, ain't you?"

"As a matter of fact, Pop, I went out. That is, I went to the museum."

"Museum, eh?" he said with benign perplexity. "What'd you do there?"

"Armor. I went with John R. Pumfret, Jr."

"Well, hey, hey. The boss's son. And how'd that come about?" He turned the ball game down even further and looked at her in a pleased and curious way.

"Pop . . . He asked me because I happened to be there, and I think—I got the impression he was lonely."

"He'll be lonely again, then," said Mr. Parrish. "That's one thing I know about lonely people. They go right on being lonely, no matter what. And have you ever noticed sumthin'? They always insist they do it best in a crowd. If I had a buck for every time I've heard some guy on television say how he was lonely in the middle of crowds, I'd own my own fleeta cabs. Beats all. Your young guy say that to you?"

"No, he didn't. And he's not my young guy, Pop. I went to the museum with him and I don't know why, and I'm sure he doesn't know why he asked me. . . . "

"He asked you because you're a pretty sweet girl, that's why."

"He asked me because I happened to be right under his nose, and I suppose he just sort of said it absent-mindedly. Or he thought he'd show me a glimpse of the higher things. He's sort of condescending, in a way."

"He is, eh? What's he got to condescend about?"

"If you ask me, very little. If you asked him, plenty."

Mr. Parrish nodded understandingly. "What's he look like?"

"A Danish pastry."

Her father guffawed. "What's that mean?"

"I don't know. His face is sort of flat and pale." She felt obscurely disloyal, without knowing why. He hadn't been much fun, or even very polite. And she had always thought of him as looking like a Danish pastry. But now she wished she hadn't said it. "I don't really mean that," she said. "He's really sort of nice-looking, in a heavy way. . . . "

"Gettin' better and better."

"Let's talk about something else."

"Sure, sure," he said agreeably, and put Mr. Pumfret, Jr., from his mind without another thought. "Whatcha gonna do now, honeybunch?" He turned a rekindled eye toward the radio. "Did that Musial make another run? I tell you, the guy's one of the seven scenic wonders of the world."

Scenic wonders? Miranda thought. Sometimes Pop's English is as bad as Mr. Pumfret's French. But her feeling for her father was all kindness. He'd only gone through the fifth grade, but had, he said, a feeling for words. "Maybe I get them a bit mixed up," he'd said once, in a rare admission. "But, still, I got this *feelin'* for them. Now, my old man never went to school at all. He spoke a straight Cockney. I'm better'n him, and you and Barney are better'n me. No tellin' where this family'll end up, keep goin' the way we are."

31

Miranda got up now and kissed him lightly on his thin hair. "I'm going to call Jenny," she said.

"Okay, honeybunch. You do that."

The ball game went up as Miranda left, and she thought, My father is a happy man. Even if he grumbles a lot, even if he and Mama have those awful fights, he's a happy man. She thought maybe it wasn't sensitive of him to be happy in spite of the frequent (long ago frightening, but now only awful) quarrels with Mama. He went into them and came out without seeming to react at all. And Mama never appeared to get really enraged. Just flushed, and louder than she was at any other time. They battled over nothing, just nothing, and stopped as easily as if they'd been actors playing a part.

Miranda had come, over the years, to accept the quarrels as she accepted bitter winter weather, or illness, or the nervous feeling the fire sirens in the night gave her. These things weren't nice. They were awful. But they weren't frightening, they weren't directed at you personally.

"I think," she'd said to Barney one day, after a particularly unpleasant quarrel that Mrs. Parrish had terminated by asking her husband what he wanted for dinner, "that they fight practically the way other people have conversation. I mean, it just about *is* their conversation, isn't it?"

"Yeah. Conversing with knives in their teeth."

"Barney, they *need* each other."

"I think you can need someone you hate."

"Don't use words like hate," she'd said with a shiver. "Anyway, I don't think you *can* hate someone you need."

"Don't you?"

"No, I don't. You're right most of the time, but you aren't right about this," she'd insisted loudly.

"I didn't say they *only* hated each other. Besides, maybe there's a little hate in all of us. We just don't all show it the way they do."

Miranda, without an answer, had walked away and left him rearranging sheet music on his stand. Now she dialed Jenny's number without much hope of finding anyone home at this hour and was pleasantly surprised to have Jenny answer.

"Oh, you're in," she said. "How come?"

"I decided to dye my *hair*. Where've you been? I *called* you."

"Pop didn't say. What do you mean, dye your hair?"

"Blonde."

"You already are a blonde."

"Wait'll you see *this*. For that matter, wait'll *I* see it. It isn't done yet. It's going to be that beigey-silver, *you* know."

"Gee. I wonder if I could do it."

"Your hair's too dark. You could do *red,* of course."

"I hate dyed red hair. I don't care how old you are, it makes you look at least nine years older and as if you'd been shellacked besides."

"How about black? Give you that Spanish look."

"No," said Miranda reluctantly. "But I'd better come

33

over and watch how yours comes out, don't you think?"

"That's why I called you. Where've you *been?*"

"Working."

"On Saturday? How *ghastly.*"

"It seems to be everybody's opinion."

"Well, natch. I mean, naturally. Look, I have to hang *up.* I'm *sizzling,* or something. My head is. Why don't we go to a movie tonight?"

"Okay."

She decided to take a quick shower and change her dress, and while she was putting on her make-up heard her mother come in and walk, heavy-footed, down the hall. "Hi, Mama," she called.

"Hello, honey. Going out?" Mrs. Parrish stood in the door, flopping a handkerchief at her florid face, puffing a bit. "Elevator's broke again."

"That's a shame, Mama." Even two flights of stairs were too many for overweight Mrs. Parrish. "I'm going over to Jenny's. We're going to a movie, maybe."

"That's nice. Wish I could get your father to take me, fat chance."

"Why don't you ask him?"

"Why don't I ask him to take me to Paris, France?"

"Oh, Mama . . . maybe he would. Take you to a movie, I mean."

"I'm too tired to go out, anyways. Where've you been all day?"

"Working," Miranda said, changing things from her tan purse to her white.

"Poor kid," said her mother feelingly, but without curiosity or outrage. She's such a relief sometimes, Miranda thought. "Gawd, how I hate to cook on a night like this," Mrs. Parrish was going on. "You wouldn't run over to the delly for me, would you? Get some cold cuts and potato salad . . . or macaroni, maybe, we had potato last night . . . and some water rolls and get a quart of milk while you're at it, okay?"

Miranda hesitated. "I don't have much money," she said. She gave a stipulated amount to the household fund, but Mrs. Parrish had a way of absent-mindedly borrowing and forgetting to pay back.

"Go ask your father."

Miranda went down the hall and explained her errand.

"We gonna have that junk again tonight?" Mr. Parrish growled, reaching for his hip pocket. "Whadda we keep a stove for? Like it's some sort of decoration? A momentum of the ice age?"

"Ice age?" Miranda said with a grin.

"Well, some bygone time. Here y'are. Cripes. If I was an anarchist, first thing I'd do is I'd blow up all the delicatessens."

Miranda gave him a noncommittal smile. "I'm going to Jenny's, Pop. So probably I won't see you till tomorrow."

"Okay, honeybunch. Have a good time."

"How are the Cards doing?"

"Behind," he said with gloomy relish. "I got this knack for pickin' losers. They lost four straight this week. Even Musial can't play nine positions."

"Still, they are in sixth."

"Yeah. No gettin' around that. Until tomorra, maybe. Maybe tomorra they'll get around it."

Miranda patted his shoulder. "So long, Pop."

"So long. Have fun."

As she went out the door, Mrs. Parrish called, "Oh, and Miranda, some oleo and one of those lemon layer cakes Barney likes, okay?"

"Sure, Mama."

She ran down the stairs, walked the two blocks to the delicatessen, waited awhile to be served. When she got back to the apartment, she could hear her father and mother yelling at each other over the ball game.

" . . . what about *me?*" Mrs. Parrish was demanding. "What about me, me, me? What do I get outa life, I ask you, stuck in the apartment day in and day out, working for you and the kids and never even a movie or nothing to get my mind offa things—"

"Workin'!" her husband shouted. "Workin' at *what,* I'd like to know. I'd like to know just what little thing it is you do around here like maybe mend a sock or pick a piece of dust offa the floor, or *cook?* I ain't had a meal since the thermometer got over sixty last May that didn't come from that damn delly. Whadda ya talkin' about, workin'? Or is it workin' when you sit around people's houses jawin' all day? Is—"

"I work, and I been working my whole life, and if it gets hot and I want a little rest from it all . . . not that I'm asking for a vacation or nothing fancy like that, you big mouth . . . just a little rest from working all the time for you and the kids, why, what do I get? Fights and screaming and yak, yak, yak. I'm tired—"

"Shush. Wait a minute." Mr. Parrish turned up the ball game. "How d'ya like that. Those *clowns* . . . they couldn't fight their way out of a barn door. . . . "

Miranda sighed and walked down the hall. She would have liked to leave without a word, but it seemed too impolite. So she went in to say good-by and found her father absorbed in the game again, her mother leaning out the window as if she'd been there for hours.

Crazy, Miranda thought. Sometimes I think they're crazy. "I'm going," she said.

Her father looked up. "Thought you already had." There wasn't a sign in his voice or on his face to show he'd just been shouting at his wife, and Mrs. Parrish turned from the window amiably, a woman who might have had a fight with her husband once, but not a serious one and surely a long time ago.

I don't understand them, Miranda thought, and I never will. But when I get married there will never be quarrels in my house. No matter what happens, no matter *what,* there will be none of this—this bitterness that passes and returns like some awful disease.

"I got the stuff, Mama."

"Did you put it away, like a good girl?"

Miranda nodded. "Well," she said again, "I'm going."

"Have a good time," her mother said. Mr. Parrish merely nodded, as if he felt he'd sped her on her way often enough. "I never," he'd sometimes say, "knew a girl took such a time gettin' out of a place. Miranda, I'd hate to pry you out of a burnin' buildin'. We'd both be up in smoke before you made a move."

Miranda had once asked Jenny Benton, "Do you ever notice that I don't say good-by to people quickly? I mean, that it takes me time to get it said, and all?"

"*Notice* it?" said Jenny. "How could I not notice it? Sometimes I wonder why you don't give up and stay wherever you're at for *good*. But I *like* it, mind. It's like —as if—you don't really want to *leave* people, or something. Very sweet, actually."

Miranda now lingered yet another minute before starting for Jenny's. Sweet? She wondered. It was nice to be thought sweet, but it seemed to her more a case of not ever really knowing if the other person was ready to have her leave.

As if, she thought, my staying or going was always up to somebody else. A *fine* way to be.

Chapter Four

JENNY'S HAIR was covered with a print scarf. She wore shorts and a halter and was smoothly tan from sessions on her own rooftop and that of the magazine she worked for. Except that her nails were bitten, she was a very attractive girl. Miranda could never bear to look at Jenny's hands, because they looked like a miserable child's and the rest of her looked like a very smart young woman. She was the only girl Miranda knew who wore hats.

"I *like* hats," Jenny would say. "Besides, I'm going to be a professional woman. Hats are part of it." Generally she would then look quickly at her nails and away. She wouldn't say anything, but you could feel her decide to stop biting them. Professional women didn't bite their nails. But Jenny went right on biting hers, and went right on looking at her hands rather the way a mother would look at a pair of children who kept getting sick for no reason anyone could find out.

They went into Jenny's room, which was made up as a

study. Miranda's room was a bedroom, because she owned a dressing table that had once belonged to her mother. She always made up in the bathroom, because the light on the dressing table was so bad, but still it was there. And her bed had both a headboard and a footboard. No way to make that room into a study.

Jenny had a couch against the wall, fitted with a tailored corduroy cover, and strewn with little bright cushions. She had an old teacher's desk, painted black with white knobs, an uncomfortable chair she referred to as a Boston rocker, and one good chair. She had brilliant travel posters from Italy and France on the walls. Jenny worked as a typist on a women's magazine, but she, unlike Miranda, knew precisely where she meant to go from there. She was going to be an editor one day, and part of her job was going to take her traveling in Europe.

"Why don't you be an airline hostess?" Miranda had asked her. "That's a way to travel. I'll bet you could be."

Jenny had wrinkled her nose. "They're just waitresses up in the *air*, aren't they? *That's* no career. I know what I'm doing."

Most of the time Miranda was pretty sure that Jenny did. What she was doing, and what she wanted. Jenny had a steady after whom Miranda had fashioned her own nonexistent one. Brad was a young salesman who was out of town a lot, and Jenny waited for him faithfully, wrote to him frequently (he wrote to her every day) and wouldn't consider going out with another man. She also admitted that she wouldn't consider, either, getting married.

She sat on the couch now, patting her scarved head. "I'm going to be sorry for *this,* I bet you."

"Maybe not. Maybe it'll be gorgeous. Can you take the scarf off?"

"Well . . . okay. All right, I mean. For a peek." She opened the closet door, where she had a full-length mirror, and carefully removed the scarf. For a long moment she stood motionless, staring at herself, before she turned and faced Miranda. "Now, for once, *don't* pussy-foot. *Do* you, or don't you?"

Jenny's hair, once the color of butterscotch, and that shiny, now looked like yellow cotton. Miranda felt a slight sinking in her stomach, wondering how long such things took to grow out.

"Maybe after it gets out of the pin curls—" she began.

Jenny looked grim. "Trying to get a straight answer out of you is like trying to make a *moth* fight back. It's horrible, now, isn't it?"

"It'll look better when you get it brushed, and all, Jenny."

"You know what *I've* got? This feeling that I'm going to have to take Monday off and go to a beauty parlor and get it all dyed *back* again."

"You could've tried tint, couldn't you? Instead of dyeing it."

"I *could've*. Miranda, just thank your stars you'll never know what it's like to be an extremist."

"All right. And you thank yours you'll never know what it is to be a compromiser."

"Shall we have a moment of star-thanking? Good. Is it over?"

"All over. I declare, I feel exceedingly refreshed."

Jenny sighed, put a thumb in her mouth, quickly snatched it away. "What were you working for, for goodness sakes? Make it long and *in*teresting, will you? I'm not really interested in a thing but my hair, but maybe you can *divert* me."

"The working part wouldn't divert you, but maybe this will. . . . I went to the museum with the boss's son."

Jenny sat up. "Di*vert* me? You *slay* me. You mean that big lump that thinks the Princeton Club is where God spends his weekends? That boss's son? The museum?"

Miranda moved restlessly, and nodded.

"And his sister hasn't ever learned your name in all the time you've *worked* there, that boss's son? Honestly, I *hate* snobs. Maybe there are some other things I hate as much as snobs, but at the moment I can't call *one* to mind. Not even that awful stuff called tripe. Which, as a matter of fact, they put me in mind of. How in the world did you happen to go out with him? You said the museum. Which museum?"

"The Metropolitan."

"Oh, well, that's all right. I've been there my*self*."

Miranda smiled

"No, but how did you happen to go with him at *all?*" Jenny persisted.

"He asked me. I didn't have anything else to do, so I went."

"So has Mr. Camp asked you. Not to the *museum,* I grant you, but the poor man's asked you out, and I don't think it's right to—"

"Jenny," Miranda interrupted. "Mr. Camp could reach my chin if he stood on his tippy toes."

"If you're going to say yes to a man just because he's tall, heaven knows *where* you'll wind up. I mean, the race is getting bigger all the *time.*"

"It's really true, you know. You should see those armors. *Every*body was Mr. Camp's size in the Crusades."

"Is that what you looked at?"

"Yes. And swords and daggers and . . . that sort of stuff."

"What else did you do?"

"Had a sandwich and some coffee."

"Where?"

"In the museum."

"But that's a cafe*teria.* Couldn't he have taken you to the Plaza, or something?"

"He could have. But he didn't." Miranda recalled her own disappointment in the cafeteria, but she'd certainly never thought of the Plaza. It would take Jenny and her publishing-world knowledge to think of something like that.

"*Then* what did you do?"

Miranda hesitated, but there was no way out of the answer. "He dropped me at the subway."

"In a taxi? He was going back to the Princeton Club?"

"In his car," Miranda confessed. "He was going back to Westchester."

Jenny opened her mouth in theatrical astonishment. "He was going right up past here, not two blocks away, and he dropped you at a subway? After dragging you all around that *armor?*" She waited to give Miranda a chance to affirm this. "Oh, big deal," she said slowly. "Big *deal.* Miranda, haven't you got any pride?"

"I have pride. Maybe that's what keeps me from asking a man to drive me somewhere when he doesn't offer. Even if he does have a sky-blue convertible," she added with a touch of wistfulness.

"Pride, dear, requires that a girl get treated . . . genteelly."

Miranda laughed. "I won't be going out with him any more, so what difference does it make?"

"Suppose he asks you again."

"He won't. He just happened to be feeling sorry for himself. Or maybe lonely," she added, recalling the pale young face so out of place behind his father's desk. "I just happened to be there at the same time, that's all. I feel sort of sorry for him."

"You feel sorry for *every*body."

After a short pause Miranda said, "Do you know what I'd like better than anything else in the world?"

"I'd be *fas*cinated to know."

"A lemonade. A big one, with maybe an ice cube here and there, and a cherry."

"That's the trouble with you," Jenny said, getting up.

"You're just *too* easy to please. It's a pity you didn't dye your hair, instead of me dyeing mine. Then when it turned out this way you could say it was just the way you wanted it all along."

I'm not that easy to please, Miranda thought. "When's Brad getting back?"

"Oh, golly. Don't mention it. He'll take one look and drop me flat. Now I'm going to *have* to wear hats. Look, let's have the lemonade, and then get dinner. I made us a shrimp salad. There isn't going to be anybody here but you and me. And then I'll take the pins out of my hair and we'll see what horrors I've done."

"Have you heard anything from him?" Miranda asked, when they were sitting at the kitchen table eating their salad.

"Now, you know I've heard from him. To tell you the truth, I sometimes wonder if I wouldn't rather hear from him than see him. That's awful, isn't it? But, you know, he *gets* here, and we're awfully glad to see each other, and we have loads to say the first evening, and maybe the next, but . . . I don't know . . . something happens. I mean, I live my life when he's away, and I have things to do. It isn't that I want any other man, or anything. I *adore* Brad. And I must say I'm awfully possessive about him. I'd get the weeps if he even *looked* at anybody else. But it's just that I'm so wild to get ahead in business, and he doesn't even want to *talk* about it. My job, I mean. He talks plenty about his, of course. But that's the way Brad is. His work is important because he figures we'll get married and he'll be the breadwinner, but my job seems to be some sort of *toy,* or *pas*time, or something." She poked at her salad a moment, resumed eating it.

"Well, you *are* going to get married, aren't you?"

"I don't want to think about it. Maybe that's why we get so . . . pe*cu*liar after a few days. Brad and I. He wants to talk about getting married, and I don't. Maybe he'll hate my hair and jilt me," she said with a smile that was almost a frown.

"He won't jilt you."

"No. Still, I don't know. *What* we're going to do, I mean. I told him the other day I'm going to go to college at night next year—"

"You are?" said Miranda with surprise. "What for?"

"Well, I just want to. I'm going to study art appreciation and music appreciation and book appreciation. You know, Miranda, I'm not really the least *bit* cultured. I mean, cultivated. One of the editors told me it's more *cultivated* to say cultivated. And I want to know about these things. The editors talk about art and books all the *time.* How am I going to be an editor if *I* can't? And do you think Brad was pleased? He acted as if I was —were— de*sert*ing him. In a way. I don't know how to explain it. But sometimes I wish that Brad and I could just go on writing letters for a few years, and *then* worry about getting married."

"Maybe you don't want to marry him at all."

There was a long silence. "Oh, I'll marry him, all right," Jenny said finally. "It's all *settled.*"

She didn't really answer me, Miranda thought. Maybe she can't.

They washed up the dishes, debated about a movie, decided against it, returned to Jenny's room.

"I suppose," Jenny said in a nervous voice, "I'd better get these pin curls out. Why did I ever *do* this?"

"Well, why did you?"

"Because one of the fashion editors, she's my favorite editor, had hers done, but she went to Charles of the *Ritz,* and of course it looks marvelous on her. Miranda, I absolutely *hate* being poor. There now, I knew I'd think of something I hated more than snobs, except I'd never be a snob. If I had money, I mean. *Making do* is the worst expression in the *world,* and it's what we're having to do all the time."

"I know," Miranda said. Making do with cheap clothes, cheap apartments, unbeautiful imitative surroundings. Knowing that the closest you'd ever get to foreign lands or lovely possessions or sophisticated conversations about— well, she couldn't think what they'd be about, but something pretty grand—was when you went to the movies. What a secondhand way to live.

"I'd like something beautiful in my life to be *first-*hand," she said.

"Meaning what?"

"Well . . . like that blue convertible. Getting a ride all the way home in it would have been firsthand. Being dumped at the subway was secondhand."

"You should have asked him. You're *too* timid."

47

"Well, I couldn't ask him. Anyway, asking would have been secondhand. What I would have liked was if he'd said, 'Now, where do I take you?' As if there was no question. Or if he'd taken me to the Plaza, the way you said. Things like that just don't happen. But it's what I mean." She laughed suddenly. "Poor little working girls."

"It's no laughing matter," said Jenny.

When the pin curls were out and the new beigey-silver hair was brushed and combed, it didn't look too bad. They examined Jenny from every angle and decided it wasn't terrible.

"Just if nobody *touches* it," said Jenny. "It feels like a *ski* cap. Oh, my . . . and it used to be so silky. I'll bet my father hits the ceiling."

"Where is he?"

"At his Saturday poker game, where else?"

"Don't he and your mother ever go anywhere together?"

"Not to my knowledge. Of course, they don't *yak* at each other, the way your parents do," Jenny said frankly. "It's just that they seem to like it better when they're going in opposite directions. You know, my mother," she mused, "is a really *intell*igent woman. I mean, I think Mother could have done *any*thing, if she'd had any education. Or if she hadn't married Pa—I mean, Dad. Sometimes I think my mother could have been a *governor,* or something. The way she practically *runs* the Democrats around here. That's where she's been all day, over at the Club, sending people out to canvas. They couldn't do a thing over there without my mother."

Miranda was more interested in marriage than the Democrats. "Do you know any married people who seem to be good for each other, or nice to each other?"

Jenny said, "You have an absolute *thing* about people quarreling. If you don't watch it, you'll wind up married to some jellyfish, telling yourself it's heaven just because he doesn't have the nerve to disagree with anybody. You've got to have some per*spec*tive, Miranda."

"You didn't answer my question."

Jenny thought. "My aunt and her husband got along all right."

"Got *along*. I asked if you knew any married people who *love* each other, and are good for each other. People who act as if they got married because they wanted to and stay married because they like it. Do you know anyone like that?"

"Well," Jenny said, touching her hair gingerly, "there *must* be some people who like it. You just don't *see* them much, I guess."

"I wonder," Miranda said dreamily, "if anything marvelous is ever going to happen to us."

"What sort of marvelous?"

"Oh . . . I don't really know. It gets all mixed up in my mind with a man that I can love very much, who loves me. But it isn't only a man. It's—being myself, and knowing it. And *rising* to something. Except there hasn't been anything to rise to, yet."

"Every day is a challenge," Jenny said soberly.

"Yes, ma'am. I just note that here—"

"Marvelous, to me, is the publisher calling me in and saying, 'Miss Benton, I've been scouring the country for a new Beauty Editor' . . . or any other old kind of editor . . . 'and here I find that right under my eyes the perfect choice has been working and waiting, how could I have been so blind, here's your private office and can you leave for Paris in the morning?' "

With a smile, Miranda agreed that marvelous had a lot of interpretations. But one thing it surely was—firsthand. Only, when did the marvelous in their lives begin?

Chapter Five

MIRANDA AND CONNIE were having their lunch hour on the roof. They had dragged camp chairs into some shade cast by a parapet to eat their warm sandwiches (made at home that morning) and their cold cokes from a machine on the top floor. It was an extremely hot day, and where the sun lay on the tarred roof it was sticky and thick-smelling. Downtown the skyline of Wall Street looked two-dimensional in the quivering air. The sound of traffic floated up to them, and airplanes, glinting and throbbingly low, went overhead.

Miranda squinted up as one, beautifully slender and powerful, went over, casting a shadow. When the noise of its motors had vanished, she said, "Suppose it's going to Lisbon? Or Norway? Or maybe Hong Kong . . ."

"It's headed for La Guardia," Connie pointed out.

"I always think of them as going away."

"Have you ever been up in one?"

"No."

"I was. At this little airfield up in Westchester. I and

this fellow took a ride in his car last summer, and we went past this place, it said, *Try the Sky, Five Dollars*. So this fellow—Larry—ast me did I want to, and I said sure. I wasn't sure, and my mother'd kill me. But we went up in this little airplane, all right, and I never did tell her."

"Was it fun?"

"I didn't like it. To tell you the truth, I only looked outa the thing once and I darn near died of fright, so I kept my eyes shut after that. Larry thought it was the nuts, though. Wonder what ever happened to him."

"I was talking about those big ones, really. The four-motored ones that fly over to Europe and all. Or California. That's the kind I'd like to go in, and *go* somewhere."

"Who wouldn't? Sometimes I think I'd like to go *any-place*. Sometimes I think I'll even visit my sister that lives in Pittsburgh, for Pete's sake, just so I can go *some*where. Only if I did, visit my sister, I mean, I'd have to go on a Greyhound. I can just picture saying to my mother, 'Ma, I'm off for Pittsburgh, how's it with you if I fly?' There'd be some flying done, all right. Ma, off the handle. I mean even if I saved the money my*self*. Sometimes I think of leaving home, getting a room somewhere."

"Don't you get along with your family?"

"I get along with them. They give me a pain in the neck sometimes, but then I suppose it's mutual. It's only that once in a while I think it'd be nice to be private or alone or something. I gotta share a room with my kid sister and she gets in my hair."

"I never can save any money," Miranda said. "Once I

opened a bank account at a place where it said you can start as low as a dollar, so that's where I started and that's where it's been ever since."

"Leave it long enough, it'll collect interest for you. When you're sixty, you can retire on it."

"My brother Barney saves money," Miranda went on thoughtfully.

"Brother? I didn't know you had a brother."

"He's sixteen."

"Oh."

"I'm always wondering how he does it. Saves, I mean. He has a job in a department store this summer, and during the school year he plays in a jazz band. They play for Elks and Rotaries and church dances and things, and make pretty good money. He puts most of it away, after he pays Mama—just keeps enough out for a date now and then and for sheet music."

"He a piano player?"

"Clarinet."

"That must be just dandy. My sister plays the piano. It drives me nuts."

"Barney's good. I like to hear him."

"What's he saving his money *for?*"

"He wants to go to college."

"Yeah? That's great. Where's he gonna go?"

"N.Y.U., he says. He says by the time he's eighteen he figures he can go to college days and work some at nights and get through with no help at all from Pop, which is fine because Pop couldn't help him. He's going to join a band in college, too," she said, proud of, and awed by, her brother, who made up his mind to do something and then went ahead and figured a way to do it.

They finished their sandwiches and cokes, crumpled the paper bags and put them aside with the bottles to take downstairs when the lunch hour was over. They had fifteen minutes still.

"I'm going on vacation, the end of this week," Miranda said.

"Lucky. I forgot you hadn't had yours yet. I woulda waited for mine, too, only Mr. Hondrig, he don't ask you, he tells you. Honestly, what a crummy boss. I think I'll start looking around for another job. How's old Pumpy treating you?"

Miranda shrugged.

"What about his son?" Connie pursued. "I think he's sorta cute. I think you're lucky, being in the same office with him and all. Except he's an awful snob, isn't he? I usta smile at him, when we passed in the hall or something, you know. But he just goes by with that snooty face in the air, so now I high-hat him, too. But he's cute. Don't you think?"

"He's all right." Miranda had never mentioned her brief outing with him to Connie.

"Honestly, Miranda. I think there's something wrong with you. Don't you get lonely? Don't you ever want to go dancing, or something?"

"I'd like to fall in love," Miranda said unguardedly.

"I thought you were in love with your steady. . . ."

Connie looked at her speculatively. "You know something, Miranda? I don't think you've got a steady at all, now, do you?"

"I . . . well, maybe he isn't such a steady any more," Miranda said, annoyed with herself.

"Ah . . . that's a shame. Well, whyn't you let me fix us up with a nice double date? I know lots of guys would like you. You don't want the floorwalker, I'll find someone else. It don't have to be *love* right away. Try them out. Go out and have a good time. Not that being in love isn't dandy. I like it. It keeps my weight down."

"How?"

"I get so nervous. Being in love gets me so I can't eat."

"Nothing wrong with your appetite today."

"Nope," Connie admitted. "I'm crazy about Joe, but I guess not in love any more. Too bad."

"Have you been in love often?" Miranda asked curiously.

"Oh, I'm always losing my head over some guy, but being in love—no, not so often. Have you?"

"Never," said Miranda dismally, and added quickly, "I mean, I was awfully fond of my steady, but not, you know—"

"I know. Well, if you'd let me fix you up with somebody—"

"Maybe sometime," Miranda said evasively. Connie was so persistent that it was hard to keep on refusing. And now that she'd lost her protective steady through her own forgetfulness, what was there to say? Hardly that it was

Connie's own descriptions of the men she saw that had made her say no all along. What could she say now?

At one o'clock they returned to their offices and began the afternoon's work. There was not, for Miranda, very much. Both salesmen were on the road. John Jr. was on vacation. And Mr. Pumfret was hard pressed to find enough to keep her busy. He did his best, and then about four said that he was going home.

"Be sure to lock up," he said, as he did every evening.

"Yes, Mr. Pumfret. Good night."

When he'd gone, she considered going into his office, where it was a scrap cooler. She even considered going home. There was nothing she couldn't leave, but even as she had the idea she discarded it. He'd come back for something, this one afternoon. Or he'd telephone, which he sometimes did, and Miranda had never decided whether it was to check on her or not, but he wanted his five o'clock's worth, even on a steamy afternoon like this. Other companies, big companies, even ones with air conditioning, often let their employees off early on days as hot as this.

Well, she thought, one thing I'm not going to do, and that's work any more. She got up and combed her hair, reapplied her lipstick, sat at her desk and took a magazine from the bottom drawer.

A few minutes later there was a step at the doorway, and Miranda jumped, trying to shove the magazine out of sight.

"Relax, honey, it's only me."

Connie came in, sat on the edge of the desk and grinned. "I saw old Pumpy-pompous go out a while ago, so I thought I'd run down and ask you—listen, Miranda, Joe just called an hour ago and he said could I get a girl, this fellow he knows, he went to school with in Troy—Joe's from Troy, you know—just moved into town. Joe says he's a heck of a nice guy, a draftsman, which is sort of like an architect. He wants to meet some girls. So how about it? Wanta go on a double with us tonight? Joe says he's tall. I ast especially."

It's times like this, Miranda thought, that I wish Mother had never met Father. What am I supposed to do with this girl? I don't want to go on a double with her, but if I keep on saying no, someday I'll hurt her feelings, and I don't want to do that either.

"I'm not dressed—" she began.

"So what's to keep you from going home and changing?" Connie said patiently. "The date's not till eight. You still stuck on that steady, or something?"

"No," said Miranda, and then wished she'd said yes.

"Well, then, let's call it set. I and these fellows will pick you up at your house. Joe has a car."

Miranda couldn't help smiling at her positive air. "Suppose I lived out at the end of Brooklyn. Does Joe just let you offer to pick people up anywhere?"

"Joe lets me do anything. Anyway, you always take the uptown subway, so it couldn't be Brooklyn. Where *do* you live?"

Miranda gave her the address, trying not to sound reluctant. After all, she didn't know that she wouldn't have a good time. Maybe this draftsman would turn out to be very nice.

"Now, you know I'm not guaranteeing to get you a fellow you can right away fall in love with," Connie said, getting up and smoothing her skirt. "Just someone to go out with, that's all. You oughta get out and meet people. You been waiting around too long. Was this guy, this steady of yours, something special?"

"No," said Miranda. "He had a sort of negative personality."

"And you so faithful and all." Connie clucked. "Well, give yourself a chance, that's what I say. I gotta get back or they'll be sending the cops. Toodle-oo. See you around eight."

After dinner that night Miranda, who'd eaten hurriedly, glanced at the clock and said, "I can't do the dishes tonight, Mama." Mrs. Parrish looked dismayed. "I can't help it. I have a date and I have to get ready."

"A date? Who with? The Prince of Wales?"

"Oh, Mama . . ."

"The Prince of Wales is nine years old," said Barney. "Or maybe seven."

"You know what I mean," Mrs. Parrish said. "Miranda acts like a guy's gotta be at least gold-plated. When's the last time she had a date?"

"I don't keep track of Miranda's dates."

"I can see that. You can't even keep track of your own.

Girls calling you here like I was an answering service. Well, you'll hafta help me with the dishes, Barney. After all, with the work I—"

"Okay, okay," Barney interrupted. "I'll help."

Mr. Parrish stretched his thin arms, rubbed his neck, got to his feet. "On my way," he said, yawning. "Half wish I wouldn't be called tonight." The garage at which he worked was run on the shape-up system, which meant that though he reported for work every night, he didn't always get it.

"Pop," said Miranda, "don't you fall asleep at the wheel."

"Not a chance, honeybunch. I'll wake up soon's I digest this wonderful dinner."

"A person can't cook on a day like this," his wife said. "I wouldn't ask a dog to cook on a day like this."

"Try it some night, anyways," said Mr. Parrish. "A dog might have some real good ideas."

"Funny man."

Miranda went into her room, got out a blue eyelet dress with a full skirt, examined her white shoes and found them clean enough, and went down the hall to run a bath. She tried to hum a little, but found she couldn't.

She'd seen Connie's friend Joe a couple of times. Sleek, with hair a bit too long, clothes a bit too sharp, eyes a bit too quick. Connie had introduced them. "I wantcha to meet my friend," she said, stopping Miranda in the hall after work. "This is Joe Pender. This here is my friend Miranda Parrish."

"Pleased to meetcha, Miranda," said Joe, sticking out his hand.

Miranda had taken it reluctantly, and the next time she'd seen him calling for Connie, had ducked back into her office to avoid a meeting. And now here she was, about to be in his company for an entire evening. *And* his friend's. Any friend of Joe's, she thought, is very little apt to be a friend of mine.

She was ready by ten minutes of eight, and went into the living room to wait for them.

Barney, glancing up from a magazine on jazz, whistled. "Hey, hey," he said. "You look great."

"Thank you, Barney," she said, feeling pleased. She sat down with her hands in her lap.

"You sure do," said Mrs. Parrish. "You put me in mind of myself when I was your age."

Miranda looked at her mother's huge shapeless body and tried not to show what she felt.

"I know what you're thinking, young lady," said Mrs. Parrish. "Let me tell you, I had the figure of a girl, when I was your age."

"I didn't mean anything, Mama."

"No." The fat woman sighed deeply. "Can't blame you for your thoughts. I dunno how I get so stout. God's my witness, I don't eat practically nothing." Neither of her children said anything, so she went on accusingly, "Do I? The trouble is, poor food is fattening food. It's only rich women can keep their figures. Eating steak and fresh berries all the time. Anyone could stay thin on good meat and expensive fruit. How can you stay thin on things you gotta stretch out with macaroni or bread crumbs?"

"I don't know, Mama," said Miranda. Barney had gone back to his magazine.

"Don't know what I got to stay thin for, anyways," said Mrs. Parrish sadly. "For my gay entrancing life? For the nice pretty compliments your father pays me? What for, I ask you?"

"I don't know, Mama," Miranda repeated unhappily.

Mrs. Parrish leaned forward a little. "You're a pretty sweet girl, Miranda. Don't you throw yourself away on any old dope that asts you to marry him."

"Mama, I'm not getting married. I'm going out on a date."

"I *like* the way you turn down dates and wait for something nice to come along, even if I do tease you about it, see? Why should a girl like you wind up fat and lonely like me? You wait for something special. Who's this fellow you're going out with tonight? Some nice party you met at the office?"

"Sort of."

Mrs. Parrish was too indolent to pursue the matter. "You have a good time, honey. But don't go throwing yourself away on just anybody. You'll wind up like me. God knows I wouldn't wish that on a dog."

Barney threw his magazine down and walked out of the room. They heard the front door slam, and he was gone.

"What's the matter with him?" Mrs. Parrish demanded.

"Well, after all, Mama . . . when you talk that way, you

aren't being very nice about Pop, are you?"

"I never thought of him at all," said Mrs. Parrish with complete surprise.

"Maybe that's the trouble," Miranda mumbled.

"I heard you. Miranda, as woman to woman, let me tell you something. Your father's a good man. Maybe I don't act all the time like I know it, but I know it. He's a good man. But I want you to have something better than the kinda life I've had. Good man or not, what kinda life has your father given me?"

What about the other way around? Miranda thought. But, then, people almost never say, What have I given? What have I gotten, what's in it for me, what kind of a life have I had? . . . Those were the questions. And it isn't only Mama, she thought. It's just about everybody. Including, let's don't forget, me. I don't like my job, and I don't like my social life, and most of the time I don't like the look of the future, but how many times do I wonder if there's something wrong with *me* that it isn't any better?

"I was just as pretty a girl as you, whether you believe it or not," Mrs. Parrish was going on. Miranda, who did not consider herself especially pretty, was quite prepared to think her mother probably had been. "Every bit as. I had dreams, too. I was gonna be better than how I was raised, and was gonna marry somebody grand and be the best wife ever. And then along came your father. So I married him. What the heck did I know about what it was gonna be like, being a hackie's wife? Twelve hours a day, seven days a week, except when he gets sick or not called, which—knock wood—he don't hardly ever. When did your father take a vacation, I ask you? When did he ever take me anywheres except once to Asbury Park twenty years ago?"

"But, Mama . . . he can't help it. Do you think Pop *wants* to work this way?"

"I'm saying it's the kinda man he is. A hackie, and he couldn't be nothing else. Why couldn't he a got in something that at least had a union, with paid vacations and minimum hours and *salaries*, like other people? Oh, no, not your father, not him—"

Miranda stopped listening, as well as she could. It was old, sad, familiar territory, and no way to say who was right or wrong or if anybody was. But not for me, she thought. Not for me. My life is going to be different. It's going to be—

She realized that it was eight-thirty, and began to hope they were going to stand her up.

"I wonder where Barney's gone," Mrs. Parrish said suddenly. "I hope he ain't gonna be mad at me."

"He's not mad, Mama. He just gets upset when you talk about Pop that way."

"I tell you, I wasn't *talking* about your father. I was—"

The buzzer rang.

" 'Scuse me, Mama." She got up and went to push the answering bell. She opened the hall door and waited a minute. The elevator didn't start, nor was there any sound of mounting footsteps. She waited another few seconds, went back to the living room and looked out the window. An old car was parked at the curb, and Connie's red head was thrust out a front window. She was looking anxiously upward, and when she spied Miranda, waved vociferously.

"They're waiting for me," Miranda said, turning into the room.

"Fine thing. That the kinda fella you got around your office? Can't even come upstairs and call for his date?"

"Mama, no." Was it worth while to explain that neither of these men worked in her office building? She decided not. "Maybe they think it's too hot to come in. Maybe they're in a hurry."

"Humph."

"Well, good-by, Mama."

"By. Don't know why you're going out on a work night. Keeping you up all hours when you hafta work tomorra. Don't you stay out too late, hear?"

"I'll try not to."

"Whaddya mean, try?"

"I'll do what I can. I'm just one of four people. I can't—" There was a long shriek of an automobile horn, and she went to the window, waved and turned away. "I better hurry."

"Great manners your friends have, I must say."

"Night, Mama. I'll see you tomorrow."

She lingered a moment more, and then ran.

Chapter Six

NEITHER of the men got out of the car as Miranda approached it, though the one in the rear opened the door for her. She climbed in, sat back with a nervous smile.

"We thought ya'd fell in," said Joe, by way of greeting.

"Miranda, I want you to meet our great friend, mine and Joe's," said Connie. "This is Les Peterson, of Troy, New York. This is Miranda that I was telling you about, Les."

"Hi, Miranda," said Les Peterson. "How's tricks?"

"Fine," Miranda piped.

Les laughed, patted her hand and winked at Connie. Miranda didn't even try to think why. He was what she had expected and had hoped not to find. A bit burlier, different features, but Les Peterson, practically an architect, was essentially another Joe Pender.

They started off.

"What we thought was we'd go to Palisades Park, for a starter," Joe Pender said. "That okay by you, Mirry?"

"Oh, that's cute," said Connie. "I could never think how to nickname Miranda. I mean, Miranda just isn't a nicknamy name, if you know what I mean. Mirry . . . that's real cute. I'm going to call you that from now on." She was sitting sideways, her arm along the seat, so that she had a view of both Joe and Les. Her hair, in the muggy heat, was extremely curly.

Miranda hadn't had a chance to give her opinion of Palisades Park as a starter. She wondered what would come after the starter and how late she'd get home. I hope Mama doesn't wait up, she thought, and then decided to forget about hours and try to enjoy the evening.

They drove over the George Washington Bridge. Lights on the Jersey shore and those on Manhattan shone in the black waters stretching north and south as far as they could see. Car lights went like smoothly rolling marbles along highways in the dark, and a plane, flashing red and green signals, crossed the sky far down the river.

In spite of open windows, Joe Pender's car had a musty, stale smoke odor. It also had some very serious-sounding rattles and a peculiar high-pitched horn. A fur monkey dangled against the windshield. Joe was an aggressive driver, the sort who seemed to hate every other car on the road, and their progress was accompanied by a running stream of his imprecations. Miranda, accustomed to her father's skillful, easy way at the wheel (he was the sort of cab driver who never lost his temper), watched Joe unhappily, but the other two seemed confident enough.

Connie confined her remarks to the passengers. "Joe

don't like to be talked to when he drives," she explained. "And that suits me. I like a man to concentrate on . . . well, on whatever he's concentrating on. That right, Les?" she smiled.

"Righto, and right as the perishin' rain," said Les, and winked at her again.

"You been listening to those English movies on television," Connie guessed.

"That's it, ducks. Got it in one."

Connie giggled with appreciation. She stretched her arm above her head, took a deep breath, relaxed and said, "Oh, my, the air is like wine tonight, isn't it?"

"It sure is," said Les, coming back to America.

"It's lovely," said Miranda.

Connie turned further around to see her. "You look *very* nice tonight, Mirry. Don't she look nice, Les? Didn't I tell you what a nice girl I was getting for you?"

"I'd take your word for anything," said Les. He seemed to realize that this was not an entirely lucky remark, so he added, with a glance at Miranda, "She looks great, great."

"Mirry's one of the nicest girls in our whole office building, and she practically never goes out with anybody, Les. You maybe don't realize how honored you are."

"Well, now, izzat so? Well, I feel the honor keenly." He looked, however, not at Miranda but at Connie, who nodded her bright head as if reaffirming her own judgment and gave Les a long plunging look before she faced forward again.

I shouldn't be surprised, thought Miranda, but I am, sort of. Still, the fact became clear that Connie was one of those girls who could be sincerely friendly with another girl as long as no man was about, but who faded and brightened and changed hue like a chameleon when a man was.

It's a good thing my feelings aren't involved, Miranda thought, because as far as my part is concerned, this date is about to drop to the ground and squash like an overripe plum. Probably, she decided, this was why Connie had been so persistent about having her. Probably she'd already run through the girls she knew, and unless they *wanted* to get rid of a man, they'd counted themselves out. She's scrounging around on the fringes of her acquaintances, because it's either that or be alone with Joe all the time. Miranda didn't blame her for not wanting to be alone with him for sixty seconds. If I were Connie, she thought, I'd drop him altogether. But Connie was not the sort of girl to release a bird in hand before she had another clearly in the net.

Well, she's welcome to Les Peterson, Miranda thought peevishly. Only I wish she hadn't had to drag me in in order to carry on her campaign. Funny that Joe didn't notice anything.

As the evening went on, however, it became apparent that Joe noticed. In a car he had attention only for the enemy, but out of the battle area there was little about Connie that escaped his notice.

They parked in a huge lot and made their way slowly

through the crowds to the caramel and hot dog scented, flaring, splashing, caliope-loud fair grounds. Joe and Connie walked ahead, Miranda and Les hurrying in their wake. Tinny waltz music blared and receded, changed tune but never seemed to, seemed to drown but never obliterated the high whining pitches of barkers at tents and in booths, the steady, shrieking, humming, laughing swell of human voices. Men and women and children went by with lollypops and balloons and shining, gluey apples on sticks, with pinwheels and whistling plastic birds and kewpie dolls and panda bears, and bags filled to bursting with popcorn. Great spinning wheels of chance buzzed and spun and came to rest and buzzed and spun again. There was the ominous squealing ascent of the roller-coasters and their steep thundering fall that rang with cries pitched on the tremulous rim of anguish and glee. Baseballs rained through the air and smacked down wooden bottles, and from shooting galleries came the steady clang of struck gongs and the ping of dead ducks.

Past freaks and swing boats and dancing girls and weight guessers they strolled, and Connie turned her laughing face to the couple behind her, pushed back her damp ringleted hair and danced on her plastic heels until Les could hardly answer Miranda, who finally left off talking altogether. She was not sulking, he was not being deliberately rude. There was simply no word or point of view between them to share, so they walked along in silence, keeping Joe and Connie in sight, waiting for the

other two to indicate a choice of distraction among all
these distractions.

Connie stopped suddenly before the carousel, and the
others drew up beside her.

It was tremendous, this merry-go-round. Miranda
watched its rounding course, picked a special horse, as
she always did, and thought it took longer to come,
proudly rising and falling, into her vision again than any
other horse on any other carousel she'd seen. A gold horse,
caparisoned rather like one she'd liked in the Equestrian
Court that day, he wore his wooden armor dashingly. His
trappings were scarlet, ornamented with blue and yellow
and green. His head was lifted high, lips curled away from
strong teeth, and his mane flowed backward in a wooden
tumultuous frieze. Surmounted by a little staring girl, he
sailed proudly by, rounded out of sight and eventually
came back again and past again while within the gold and
white and purple turret the band organ poured forth a
brassy, three-quarter-time march.

Miranda smiled and said, "I'd like to ride it. Wouldn't
you, Connie?"

"Mad to," said Connie. "Aren't you cute. Joe, get us
some tickets, okay?"

Joe hesitated, looked at Les. "Well, anyhow," he said
grimly, "you can pay your share."

"Oh, sure, sure." Les's hand went quickly to his hip
pocket. "Got carried away."

"Not far enough," Joe muttered, low enough so they
were free to ignore him, which they did. He went and

stood in line, darting purposeful glances every now and then at the waiting three.

"Isn't it just dreamy?" Connie said. "Honestly, I don't think anything's more fun than a fair grounds, do you?" She was looking at Les.

"Yeah," he said. "I'd rather go dancing."

Connie's eyes widened. "Oh, well, dancing, of course. That's more fun than *anything*. You ask Joe, all right, Les? Ask him when you can get him alone a minute and maybe we can go dancing later on. That'd be marvelous. There's lots of nice roadhouses around here, probably juke boxes, of course—"

"I like a juke better'n these square combos they get in places outsida New York. What I mean to do is, I'm gonna take in places in New York like the Stat and the Roosevelt. Get to dance to some real bands, now I'm in ol' Gotham herself."

"Really?" said Connie. Her lips parted and she looked up at him wistfully. "That sounds awfully cute. That sounds like something anybody'd like to do."

Les took a breath, glanced over at Joe, who was approaching, at Miranda, who was looking the other way, released his breath and winked at Connie. She seemed satisfied. She turned to Joe as if enraptured at the sight of him. "You've been but *ages*," she accused him affectionately. "If I'da known it'd take you *that* long—"

"What would you of done, I'd like to know?" he asked in a sulky tone.

"Why—" she took his arm "—I'da come and stood with

71

you, of course." She sparkled at him, and Joe relented cautiously. He put his arm around her waist, glared at Les and said, "Here. Here're your tickets. Yours and Mirry's here. Have a good ride. Tally-ho." He led a laughing Connie away. She gave them one mischievous backward look, and seemed to be growing prettier by the minute.

This is silly, Miranda said to herself, because she was feeling awkward and even hurt. Just silly. You can only be hurt by people who matter to you, and Connie and Joe Pender and Les whatever his name is don't matter to me. She stuck her chin up, because she'd discovered a long time ago that to stick your chin up in troubled times was not just an expression, it was a help.

Walking with Les through the little fenced entrance to the merry-go-round, she said to herself, "If I get that horse, everything will be all right." She wasn't sure what she meant, but she did want to get that one particular horse. Forgetful of Les, she hurried in search of her choice and saw, with a sinking heart, the little girl still perched staring on his back. She slowed up, and then—oh, joy—a man leaped to the platform and lifted the child down. Miranda made a dash, beat out a young white-clad sailor, who grinned at her, tipped his hat, walked on, turned back and said, "Want some help mounting? He's a pretty big steed."

Then Les was there, not looking particularly eager, but there. The sailor grinned again and sauntered on. He looks a heck of a lot nicer than what I'm with, Miranda thought. But, then, someone you were not with very often looked better than someone you were. She sat sidesaddle on her horse, foolishly patted his flowing mane, and waited for the ride to begin.

"The Danube Sooo Blue . . ." the band organ blared with drums and cymbals. Imperceptibly Miranda's horse began to glide upward. He descended more quickly, the carousel moved, picking up speed, the music swelled, and then they were driving swifter and swifter . . . around, around, up and down, the music crashing, lights streaking by, people flashing by . . .

It really is like flying, Miranda thought, adoring it, leaning forward, her hair lifting behind her, her horse trusty and beautiful in his flight. The forlorn feelings of a few minutes past streamed away like fog dispersing in a breeze. I wonder, she thought, why I don't remember, between one time and the next, how much I love a merrygo-round.

Around and around, to the music, to the lights, to the rushing night air her gold horse glided, lifting and descending . . . and then after a long time that was too little time, the scream of the roller-coasters, the clangor of the shooting galleries, the cry of the people filtered through the music, louder and louder. The carousel slowed, slowed, almost stopped, and then did. Her horse poised uncertainly, shivered and grew still.

No more? she wondered. This was too much stillness after flight, and though she called it nonsense, it felt like desolation.

Then Connie, signaling from a horse on ahead, indicated that she wished a second ride. Miranda smiled back at her, and waved, and waited for it all to begin again.

The unfortunate people who had to leave, left. A surge of new riders sprang to the great circle and claimed their mounts. Miranda held the reins lightly and wondered if it would be more fun to ride a real horse. She was deciding that probably it wouldn't when her idly wandering eye was arrested and she forgot about horses. In the crowd, leaning against the side of a booth of chance, was a young man she had never seen before. She was sure of that, the moment she saw him. Yet his face, his stance, his expression as he looked about him at the people were so familiar that it seemed impossible she did not know him. She leaned forward, trying to get him in the best possible focus. What *was* it about him that made him, to her, not a stranger that she had never seen before and would not again, not part of a shifting crowd that might consist of these people or of any others, but this one young man— outstanding, individual, not ever to be mistaken for anyone else? Tall, a little thin, with a grave mouth and good-humored hopeful eyes, he was not so very different from other young men. And he was a stranger. And she was on a merry-go-round that was just about to start its circular journey to nowhere. But Miranda, who hardly ever did anything on impulse, pulled her foot out of the stirrup to leap from her horse and run to him. I've been waiting for him, she said to herself calmly. I just can't ride away and leave him, now that I know . . .

Then it was too late. Her horse shuddered a little and

74

lifted and began to move forward as Miranda twisted wildly to keep her young man in view. Would he be there on the next time round? Would he be there when this ride was over, if ever this ride was over? He was there once, then twice, and then she couldn't tell because the merry-go-round carried her in a blur too bright and swift for seeing.

He was not there when the ride ended.

Miranda, sliding from her horse with a sigh, patted its wooden mane, as if in forgiveness, and joined the three unknowns to whom she was committed.

They rode the big roller-coaster. They rode through the Tunnel of Love, and Miranda laughed to herself at the way she and Les sat stiffly apart in the darkness while scary things that were supposed to send her squealing into his arms dashed out of the black and disappeared. Maybe, she decided, he isn't even here any more. Maybe he's climbed over all these people (Joe had seen to it that he and Connie were several boats forward) and pushed Joe into the canal and now he and Connie are happily planning an evening at the Stat.

They splashed into the light, and Les said, "Let's go, huh?" He did give her a hand out.

By now the sole and flaming wish in Connie's mind was that the four of them go dancing. She was overanimated with this desire, and incapable of enjoying anything else. She threw imploring glances at Les, who had apparently not had an opportunity to suggest a roadhouse, and exasperated ones at Joe, who didn't think to suggest it. She bridled and interrupted and fell silent and grew shrill. Joe, who had settled into a condition of unremitting sulkiness, merely scowled into the distance, and Les sent silent messages of helplessness.

Miranda watched them, and wondered what would happen.

"Joe," Connie burst out at last, driven to speak because they would not, "don't you think we've had enough of this? I mean, I'm mad about it and all, but my goodness, enough's enough, isn't it?" Joe looked at his watch. "Oh, my goodness, Joe, I didn't mean go *home*. . . . I mean, it's early as anything yet, but couldn't we do something different, like—oh, like maybe go dancing?" She fluttered her lashes and looked amazed. "How about *that?* What do you think, Les? Mirry, would you like to go—"

"Okay, Connie," Joe interrupted. "Why din you say so before? How'd I know what was nibbling you? You want to go dancing, we go dancing." He didn't find it necessary to consult anyone else.

"Honey, that's a marvelous idea," Connie said, surprisingly, but with utter confidence in her tactics. She leaned over and patted his cheek. "That's the cutest idea you've had." Joe gave her a dim, reluctant smile.

They walked to the parking lot, found the car and drove away. The amusement park spun and flared and glowed behind them, like a Catherine wheel receding in the night.

She got in late, and was relieved to find that her mother

hadn't waited up. She didn't want to talk any more tonight to anyone. What could she say of the evening, if asked? The date had been just a date. She hadn't minded it too much, she'd enjoyed dancing, she was glad it was over.

Could she say, "Mama, I lost something tonight"?

"Not your watch, I hope," her mother might say.

"No. The man I could have loved."

"What sort of nonsense is that? You never met this fellow before."

"I never met him at all, Mama. He was standing in the crowd and my horse took me away from him, and when I got back he was gone. So I couldn't go and tell him I'd been waiting for him all this time."

No, she certainly could not say that to her mother. And, now that she was home, away from the spell of the merry-go-round and its music, she couldn't believe she'd have leaped from her horse and run to a young man in a crowd and said, "Where have you been? I've been waiting for you. . . . "

Chapter Seven

"HOW DOES IT FEEL?" said Jenny. "Two whole weeks ahead of you with nothing to do but loll?"

"Heaven," said Miranda. "Everything is heaven. Especially this part."

Jenny didn't deny it. After this weekend Miranda would be back in the city, with little likelihood of getting away again, so naturally this weekend looked wonderful.

They were on a bus, on their way to visit Jenny's aunt, who had a house on a lake in New Jersey, and who took boarders but had said she was free of all but one this weekend and would love to have the girls visit.

Miranda had been there for a few days the summer before and, like any city-bred child, had promptly and unreservedly fallen in love with everything. The house was enormous and inconvenient and rather dark and in need of paint. It had a large veranda—facing the road, not the lake—a six-foot hedge, haphazardly trimmed, in front, and a garden in back where she and Jenny had been able to pick real currants. They'd swum in the lake, listened to crickets at night, awakened to songbirds rather than sparrows and pigeons. Miranda had even mowed a good stretch of lawn and so had smelled, for the first time in her life, freshly cut grass.

She sighed at the thought of coming pleasures and then glanced at Jenny, the provider of it all. Jenny was a generous girl, with very little means to indulge her generosity. "Except that you do," Miranda had said once. "You don't have to have money to be generous." "Oh, I know," Jenny had said ruefully, "you mean I'm generous with my*self* and my *time*. I'd like to be lavish with plain hard cash once in a while. I'd like to buy my mother a coat that was warm *and* pretty. That kind of generous."

Miranda knew what she meant. Once in a while she had daydreams of winning a lot of money in a quiz contest (what kind of quiz she could win was the hardest question of all) and going home to Pop with a suitcase full of gold. "Here, Pop," she'd say, "go out and buy yourself a taxi-cab, and drive it every other Thursday or not at all, anything you like. . . ."

"Of all the jobs in the world," she said now, "I think driving a cab is the worst."

"Lots of jobs are the worst. In fact, any job is worse than any other, if you look at it closely enough."

"Something wrong at the office?"

"I must say, Miranda, sometimes you incline to be *too* direct. Well . . . not to say wrong. It's just that I'm

79

sick and tired of being a typist. I am meant for better things than Gregg and the standard keyboard."

"You'll get them," Miranda said with soothing confidence. "Especially when you go to college nights and start appreciating all those things. You should move along rapidly after that."

"You sound like our personnel manager. Why don't you come to school with me, Miranda? Don't you want to appreciate things, too?"

"Yes. I mean, there are lots of things I'd like to appreciate already, but it just seems like too much to have to start learning. I work all day and I don't want to work at night, too."

"It isn't supposed to be work, it's supposed to be pleasure."

"I'd find it work," Miranda said firmly. "How is Brad these days?"

"Oh, my goodness . . . here I've had a letter from him in my bag since *morn*ing," said Jenny. She added quickly, "I've been *saving* it." As if she hadn't just admitted forgetting it. She opened and read it quickly, favored it with a smile of conscious tenderness, returned it to her bag and said, "I'm starved, aren't you?"

"Do you always read his letters that way?" Miranda asked curiously.

"Fast, you mean? No. And of course I'll read and reread it," she continued in a dutiful tone. She gnawed gently at her index finger and looked out of the window.

It was Friday evening, and to Miranda the office and

her job seemed inconceivably far away. Today had been boringly easy. She'd spent the morning alone, clearing up odds and ends and doing her nails. She'd had lunch with Connie, whom she hadn't seen for two days, since the night of the double date.

"I've been so busy, I can't *tell* you, in the office," Connie explained. "I haven't had a minute to breathe, and then yesterday I had lunch—I mean to say, this friend of mine came by and said would I go to lunch and all, and I didn't want to say *no*. Him wanting it so badly and all."

What's she explaining to me for? Miranda wondered. We don't have lunch together every day, and even if we did—

". . . but I did want to tell you, Miranda, the boys just absolutely thought you were a knockout, they just *raved* on the way home. Your ears musta just been burning."

Miranda looked at her, stupefied.

"No, but I was saying to Les yester—that is, I mean—" She broke off in a fluster.

"Is that who you had lunch with?" Miranda asked pleasantly.

"Yes. I . . . yes, it was Les," Connie admitted, as if she'd been caught.

"I hope you aren't worrying about me," Miranda said. "Because please *don't*. I mean, your friends are very nice, but I really don't mind in the least—"

"You don't?" Connie said dubiously.

"No, really." She added, with what she considered inspiration, "I guess I'm not really over my steady quite yet."

"Oh. Too bad." Connie gave that a respectful pause, and then rushed on, "You understand, Les was just wild about you. He said so over and over and what a good dancer you were and all, but—" She lifted her smooth shoulders, preened a little and said in a tone of shy astonishment, "—I guess it was just one of those things. I and Les. Gosh, I'm awfully glad you aren't hurt."

"I should think it would be Joe you'd be worried about."

"Oh . . . Joe. Joe's gotta face things, is all. I mean, he can't get a hammerlock on a girl, even if he'd like to, *which* he would. Not on a girl like me, anyway. Les says a guy would be crazy to expect to hang on to a girl like me."

Does that come out to a compliment? Miranda wondered. "Well," she said. "These things do happen."

Connie looked at her approvingly. "It's marvelous to talk to somebody who understands," she said.

They had lunch at a tearoom, in celebration of Miranda's last day, and Miranda ran over a mental list of things to do while Connie ran over a list of Les's wonderful points, of which there were a surprising number.

All packed, thought Miranda, except for toilet articles and my good cotton dress— "Is he? I didn't notice, but I'm sure you must be right." I mustn't forget the box of mixed nuts for Mrs. Long. Maybe I should have gotten

something nicer? "Yes, he's *very* polite. I noticed that."
Well, he did yank me out of that boat when the ride was
over. You have to take politeness where you find it. What
I'll do is, I'll get home and take a bath, and then manicure
my toenails, and after that—

"Don't you think so?" Connie was demanding.
"Miranda, pay attention.'

"I'm sorry, I—"

"Don't you think Les is the best dancer you've ever
known?"

"No," said Miranda. Connie looked outraged. "Well,
Connie, you asked me. He's a very good dancer, but . . .
well, my brother, Barney, is the best dancer I've ever
known."

"Your brother? What's the point in dancing with your
brother?"

"It's fun sometimes. He has a feeling for music. He
has a real beat."

"Well, believe me, so has Les. I'm amazed you didn't
notice it."

"But I did. I said he was a very good dancer. I only
said—"

"He is positively, with no question, the best dancer I
personally have ever known," Connie said coolly. "And
I have done some dancing in my lifetime. By now I bet
you I've danced *thousands* of miles." Her voice implied
that Miranda probably hadn't even danced hundreds.

Her coolness didn't last, because she was anxious to
explain how she and Les were going to dance to every

name band in New York City. Her eyes glowed and her voice was taut with excitement. Miranda, feeling obscurely sorry for her, wondered if Connie had any friends. The way I have Jenny, she thought, and others that I don't see as much as Jenny but like very much anyway and have a good time with. Who would want to be intimate with Connie? You'd spend all your time listening to how she had swept them off their feet, to her great surprise.

" . . . well, honestly," Connie was winding up, as she fished in her huge bag for her wallet, "I'm going to miss you something awful. It'll be dead around here without you, no kidding."

She had such a sincere expression on her insincere face that Miranda could only reply that she would miss Connie too.

About two o'clock John Jr. came in, looking cool in blue shorts. He was the only man Miranda knew who wore them to business, and the first time he'd done so she'd been so overcome she'd made four typing errors. When she inquired of Jenny, who knew all about fashion, whether this wasn't a ghastly gaffe, Jenny had said absolutely not. "Just as chic as *can* be. I *hope* he has good legs. Too dreary for you if he doesn't." He had. Brown, sturdy, slightly heavy, but good. Miranda still found it a little embarrassing. It was odd that John Jr., so humble where important things, like his rights in the office, were concerned, could be so calmly at ease in his unconventional dress. Of course, he did look correct on top. Blue cord jacket, white shirt, navy tie. Probably, Miranda had decided, he feels at ease because he feels superior. None of the other men in the building wore shorts to work, but they all envied John Jr. aloud, and threatened to do likewise.

In he walked, conventional on top, his good legs showing, and said, "Hello, Miss Parrish. This place is a tomb, isn't it?"

"Yes, Mr. Pumfret."

He gave her a doubtful glance. "I don't have a thing to do. Not a letter, not a memo, not even a phone call to ask what the devil's holding them up. Nothing." He walked into his father's office, stood a moment, hands behind his back, strolled back to the door. "But I'm here, Lafayette. On deck, at the call of, etc. Here, here I am."

So am I, Miranda thought. But of course it wasn't the same thing.

Although John Jr., since their afternoon at the museum, had never made any mention of it (although he had even, in the beginning, seemed afraid that she might), still, since that day he had in some subtle way felt free to complain to her on occasions when they were alone. He complained in a remote manner, clearly not requiring or expecting any response from her. Certainly not a sympathetic response. John R. Pumfret, Jr., did not like the knit-goods business. *I'm too good for it,* he said in all but words when he and Miranda were alone in the office. When his father was there, or even the salesmen, he was businesslike enough, though sullen and rather lazy.

Miranda was sorry for him. She hoped he had fun when he sailed, or studied his armor, or did the things he did when away from the office, because he surely took no pleasure in the business of making a living. And who am I to talk? she wondered. I don't like it here myself.

"Where's the substitute girl?" he said suddenly. "I thought she was going to come to school to you, learn the fascinating intricacies of getting the men of the land underclothed and hosed." He picked up a pencil and bounced its rubber tip on her desk.

"She was here for three days this week while you were out."

"And you taught her everything you know?"

"In three days?" she murmured, wondering if he even knew how insulting he sounded.

"I suppose I sounded sort of insulting," he said.

Miranda glanced up quickly. "Did I speak aloud?" she said. "I thought I only thought it."

There was a silence, during which Miranda told herself she'd be surprised, but not very, if he suddenly said, "You're fired."

He did surprise her by saying, "I'm sorry," before he wandered off to his desk in the showroom.

Miranda stared at her cleaned-up desk, wondering whether to write a letter so as to give an impression of working. She decided against it, but didn't have the courage to get out her magazine, so she merely sat, swiveling back and forth, wondering why it wouldn't occur to him to let them go home. Afraid his father would call, probably. I'm glad I'm not afraid of my father. She began to go over her list again, simply because it was fun to be planning a trip, even a little trip. First a bath, then her toenails—

"What are you going to do on your vacation?" He was back.

"Well, I'm going away for the weekend. And then . . . well, then I just haven't decided." She hoped it sounded as though the choices were so many that she was hard put to make one. Why she hoped this was difficult to say. Maybe because she was tired of being impressed by the sound of everything the Pumfrets did on vacations. Sailing, golf, trips to Nova Scotia. It all sounded grander than she really believed it was, but still it sounded awfully grand. "I simply can't decide," she repeated.

"Where are you going for the weekend?"

"A friend of mine's aunt's house." She regretted the ungrand sound of that the moment she said it. "She has this house, in a lake district—" *that* was better "—my friend's aunt, I mean. We're simply going for a few quiet days. We may stay longer." No need for him to know that Jenny had to be back at work on Monday and she herself was not invited to stay longer.

"That should be elevating," he said. " A quiet stay by the river's rim."

"It's a lake."

"Haunts of coot and hern."

Miranda didn't answer this. John Jr. wandered off and

for half an hour there was no sound but the whir of the big lazy fan. Then he came back and said, "There's no reason for you to hang around, is there?"

"Not really," she said, jumping up.

"Then run along," he said grandly. *"En les grandes vacances!"*

She gave him a warm friendly smile, not so much for the time off as for his thinking of it, and ran along.

She turned now to Jenny and said, "Mr. Pumfret let me off two hours early today."

"Softening of the brain?"

"John Jr."

"Oh. Has he ever said *any*thing about your afternoon together that day, or is he still pretending it never happened?"

"He never says anything, really. But he's nice and relaxed with me. Feels free to complain behind his father's back and things like that."

"Comfy. Maybe it's a sign."

"Of what?"

"That he's falling in love with you. Brad complains to me about everything. I think it's one of the ways men have of showing you that they care."

"Maybe. Except that I can't see John Jr. in love with anybody. He's . . . too full of himself, you know. There has to be a little room for someone besides yourself if you're going to love, wouldn't you think?"

"I'd think, sure. But, then, what I don't know about love is going to take me the rest of my life to get over,"

Jenny said frankly. "Every time I think I should think about Brad I find myself thinking about how to get ahead at the magazine instead." She fell into a brooding silence, and Miranda looked about the landscape, trying to see something familiar.

The bus let them off in front of a brightly lighted drugstore in the small town nearest Mrs. Long's house. For a moment they stood on the sidewalk, holding their suitcases, looking around, and then a voice was calling, "Yoo-hoo . . . Jenny . . . Miranda!" and Jenny's aunt was hurrying toward them.

"Here they are, Matt," she called over her shoulder. "Wait there. Hurry up, girls." She panted, smiled and fluttered. "Matt's over there in a no-parking place—" She herded them toward an old blue sedan parked beside a fire hydrant. "In you go, loves."

Jenny and Miranda climbed in back with their suitcases, and Mrs. Long flung herself beside the driver. "Hurry, Matt, hurry."

"For a law-abiding woman," said the man at the wheel as they started off, "you have an unreasonable fear of policemen."

"All reasonable people are afraid of policemen. Girls, this is Matthew Smith. These are my nieces, Matt. I mean, Jenny is my niece, my sister's daughter, and Miranda is her lovely friend." She forgot to give their last names. Mrs. Long was frequently forgetful and nearly always flustered.

Miranda, who'd enjoyed being called a niece, tried to

make out the driver, but could only see that he was young and probably tall.

"I was going to pick you up myself," Mrs. Long was saying, "but Matt said no, no, he wouldn't think of it—"

"I said you might as well stay alive as long as I'm around." He had a nice voice, deep and a little scratchy. A voice you'd remember.

"Matt thinks I don't drive very well," Mrs. Long explained unnecessarily. "Of course, I'm perfectly competent, as long as the other drivers know what they're doing, but anyway, here we are. We've done all the marketing, and won't have to stir all weekend. Except Matt, of course, who can't stop stirring when he isn't working. Working on his book, I mean. He's putting up kitchen shelves for me—all his own idea, *I* wouldn't have asked—but you two are just to relax and rest. When I *think* of you slaving away in that dreadful city—"

"Aunty, I love the city," said Jenny, as if in defense of a prized possession.

"That's right, isn't it? I keep forgetting." Mrs. Long leaned over the front seat and peered at her niece. "What do you have on your head, dearie?"

"My hair," Jenny said on a bursting giggle.

"Your hair?" Mrs. Long was practically in the back with them, looking. "My dear girl, your *hair?* What happened to it?"

"I dyed it."

"Whatever for?"

"I was trying to be chic."

Mrs. Long clucked and subsided to her seat. "You look as though you'd had a terrible fright. Oh, well, it'll grow out. I dare say it doesn't look *too* bad. Just surprising. What does your mother think? How *is* she, Jenny? My, it seems a long time since I've seen her."

"She's fine, Aunty. Working hard at her job and hard at the Democrats and looking lovely."

They went on talking family matters, and Miranda slid over in her seat, trying to get a good look at Matthew Smith. Working on his book, Mrs. Long had said. A writer, then? That was sort of exciting.

Through the open car windows the evening air, faintly cool, faintly fragrant, moved against her face, and it didn't seem a year since she'd been here last. A year. And what had happened? She'd gotten a year older. Well, something more than that. She'd looked for a job and found one, and learned to do it without learning to like it. Was that progress? There must be, she thought, a lot of people who get a job and learn to do it without liking it and never do anything else the rest of their lives, and that must be awful. Of course, women are more apt to have things change than men are. Even if men marry, they still have the job, and maybe still don't like it but can't do anything about it. Women can quit work and have children. Miranda thought it would be lovely to have children, but how could she get married if she never fell in love? And how could she fall in love if she never met anyone to fall in love with?

How could you fall in love if the people you met were

John R. Pumfret, Jr., and Les Peterson, and an occasional leftover from high school who called because he "just happened to run across your number in his book"?

Miranda felt, on this the first night of her vacation, faced with the recollection of the past year and the dim view of a stranger's profile in the front seat, almost wildly abused. I want something beautiful to happen, and nothing ever happens at all, she told herself rebelliously.

"Well, and Miranda, how have you been?" said Mrs. Long.

Miranda started. "Just fine, Mrs. Long. I've been just fine. It's lovely to be on vacation, though. And lovely to be here."

"I'm so glad you could come," said Jenny's aunt. Her voice was fluttery and sweet and kind. She was a widow, and she had to keep a boardinghouse, and she didn't have any children. But she always sounded to Miranda like a happy person.

When they arrived at the house, Matthew Smith carried their bags up to the big room, facing the lake, which they'd shared the year before.

"That," said Jenny when he'd gone, "is a *wildly* personable young man."

"Isn't he?" Mrs. Long perched on one of the beds. "And such a *nice* one. He's staying here all summer and doing repairs around the place. I'm not charging him, of course. Really, I don't know which of us is getting the best of the bargain."

"What does he write?" Jenny asked.

"He's written some short stories. Sold them, too. But now he's writing a novel. He's hoping he'll finish it this summer. He writes mornings and works around the house afternoons, and writes sometimes in the evening again. He's *very* disciplined," she said in a wistful tone.

"Doesn't he have a job?" Jenny asked.

"Oh, yes. He's a moving-man. All those muscles, didn't you notice? Very handy, too. But he just took the summer off, to finish his novel. He's been working on it for three years. *Imagine.*" She patted her knees a couple of times, got to her feet. "When you're finished washing up, come down and we'll have a late supper. I know you must be starved. Or are you living on fingernails, Jenny?" She gave them each in turn her misty smile and drifted away.

"I wish people would stop *nagging* me about my nails," Jenny complained. "You'd think I wasn't already miserable enough, you'd think I wanted to— What's the matter with you?"

Miranda, who hadn't spoken since they entered the house, was sitting on the window seat, watching a ragged-winged moth implore entry at the screen. He wasn't going to get in, and he wasn't going to give up, and Miranda wondered briefly whether, as far as the moth was concerned, this was good or bad. To have an aim he could not realize, or to have no aim at all?

Matthew Smith was not the young man she'd seen from the merry-go-round that night. For a moment or two, when he'd gotten out of the car, she'd felt her blood quicken and her head swim, thinking that, incredibly, against all chance, she had found him again. Then, when she looked more closely, she saw that it was not he. Only something about him, something in his carriage, in the expression on his face, was the same. Could it be that there was a *sort* of person you fell in love with? That you recognized right away?

Suddenly the moth, in his flutterings, dropped below the window and, once free of the light, disappeared into the garden. Miranda turned back to Jenny, who was fretting at the door, and agreed that they should go down to Mrs. Long and Matthew Smith.

She had fallen in love. There was no doubt in her mind about that at all. But she didn't think she'd be able to do anything about it, and she certainly couldn't tell anybody. Maybe, after the weekend was over and she'd gone back to the city, she'd get over it and gradually forget. Meanwhile, like that moth, she'd found the light she yearned for and she fluttered toward it.

Chapter Eight

THE FOLLOWING MORNING she awakened at six. A trip to the bathroom disclosed no sound in the big house except the deep steady ticking of an old wooden-framed wall clock on the landing. She went back to bed and lay, listening to the birds. Jenny, peacefully curled beneath a light blue blanket, slept on, and it seemed that ages passed. When the clock struck the half-hour, Miranda got up, dressed silently and crept downstairs.

Matthew Smith was coming through the hall, yawning. He stopped when he saw her and said, "Well, this is nice. Company for coffee. I didn't know working girls got up so early when they weren't working."

Sensing approval, Miranda saw no reason to tell him that at home getting up was the cruelest part of the day, and yet she did tell him. It seemed in some way important that, however briefly he knew her, he should only know what was true. "I hate getting up in the morning," she said, following him into the kitchen. "It's just . . . here, somehow. I don't like to waste it."

"I know," he said, pouring orange juice and measuring coffee into a percolator, while Miranda's doting eyes followed his every move. "I like the city very well, but somehow it's harder to get up and face the day to the muttering of pigeons and sparrows than to . . . well, whatever the birds are around here. Very musical and arousing."

He turned and Miranda quickly dropped her glance. She put her finger in the bowl of a spoon, twirled it around and at length looked up with more composure. Falling in love so suddenly and completely after years of wondering what all the talk was about was to her a most tremendous matter, but it could not be so to Matthew Smith, and he was not to know about it. She had no doubt that many other girls and women (he must be at least twenty-five) had loved him, and the chances were that one did now. The probability was that he loved her back. Men like Matthew just didn't wander around heart-whole and free, did they?

"I've never met a writer before," she said, sipping her orange juice and wondering if her voice sounded as breathless as she felt.

"Don't be too sure you've met one now."

"But Mrs. Long *said.*"

"Mrs. Long is generous. What she means is, I write."

'Isn't it the same thing?"

He gave her a wistful half-smile and shook his head. "Not necessarily."

"What do you write about?"

He hesitated, and then said, "I don't mean to sound inaccessible, but I just don't know how to talk about it. Sometimes, when you've been working on a thing as long as I have this book, it gets to be like a familiar."

"A familiar?"

"That's a sort of personal ghost. You can't get rid of it, and you're used to it, but it sort of gives you the creeps. I can't even put the thing out of my mind when I try to. It's like throwing away a feather. Have you ever tried to throw a feather away?"

"No," said Miranda, and laughed. "Is it hard?"

"It's hard. That's the way I feel about my book half the time. A lightweight thing that I can't throw away even for a minute. Well—" he got to his feet "—this has been fun, but I have to work now. I'm glad you get up early."

"So am I."

He turned at the door and said, "By the way, are you any good as a carpenter's assistant?"

"I could try," she said in a voice so eager that she blushed. She felt her face redden and ignored it, as if it were happening to someone else. "I'd like to try," she said resolutely.

"That's fine. You can hold the boards while I saw them. You'll be a nice change from my foot."

Oh, golly, she thought while she did the few dishes they'd left, what if I hadn't gotten up? What if I was still in bed, asleep and dreaming something lovely, instead of awake and *having* it?

"Good morning, dearie." Mrs. Long flitted in. "How

are you this morning?"

"Oh, I feel wonderful. Just wonderful."

"That's fine. It's the country air," Mrs. Long pointed out. "There is nothing like country air to make a person feel good."

"No," said Miranda. She could not stop smiling.

There was no sign of Matthew Smith for the rest of the morning. Jenny came down, yawning and rubbing her eyes, at nine-thirty and squinted at Miranda, who was cutting up string beans. "Didn't you ever go to *bed?*" she mumbled.

"Yes. But not to spend the weekend there. I want to see the birds and the bees and things. I picked all these beans, and besides that I took a walk along the lake, and I'm going to help Matthew Smith saw wood this afternoon—"

"Miranda, stop. Wait'll I've had my coffee."

"I was only telling you all the happy things."

"A kind word, a few spools on a string, and Miranda's satisfied. Like a *baby*. Honestly. Where's Aunty?"

"In the basement, getting stores. Because of all the people coming next week, and the woman who works here isn't here this weekend. Jenny, thank you for asking me up."

"You're supposed to say that at the end of the weekend, I *think*."

"Well, I'll say it then, too. Jenny, when I finish these beans, let's go swimming, all right?"

The water was cool and, near the land's edge, quite

marshy. But Mrs. Long had had a little jetty built, and they walked to the end of this and sat in the drenching sun poking a toe in the water now and then, waiting to be hot enough to plunge. Neither Miranda nor Jenny could swim well, and they couldn't dive at all, but the longer they waited the more inviting the lake became. At length they climbed down the ladder and launched off.

"Oh, but it's *marvelous*," Jenny gasped, ducking and splashing and shaking the drops from her matted hair. "Isn't it?"

Miranda flailed her arms in a blissful, inexpert crawl. It's heaven, she told herself. Everything's heaven.

Later they lay face down on the warm wooden planks, listening to the low gurgle beneath the jetty. There were boats out on the lake, and people swimming from nearby houses. Sounds of radios and lawnmowers and voices filled the hot high morning.

"Just think," she said to Jenny, from the hollow of her arm, "there are people who stay here all *summer*."

But Jenny, once again, was asleep.

Mrs. Long recalled them to the house with threats of sunburn and promises of lunch, and they went upstairs to get ready.

The room they had was large, with random-board floors on which were a few small hooked rugs. The furniture was worn maple, and on the spool beds were hand-made patchwork quilts. "Aunty makes them," Jenny had explained. "She sews away at them winters, and sells them in the summer through some person who has a market on

the highway." Mrs. Long, for all her flyaway air, seemed
to work all the time. She ran the boardinghouse with the
help of one daily woman, she gardened, and put up the
fruits of her garden, and sewed, and heaven knows what
else she does, Miranda thought, that I don't even know
about.

"Are you really going to help carpenter this afternoon?" Jenny asked, frowning at herself in the mirror.
"You know where he'll probably be working? Out in the
barn. It's a garage now, but it still smells like hay and it
gets in your nose and it's *broiling*."

Miranda, who saw only the delights, said, "You can
come along, if you like, Jenny." Little as she wanted
company this afternoon. Jenny was her good friend and
not to be excluded from such a joy as holding boards for
Matthew Smith in a hot barn on a hot afternoon.

Jenny lifted one brow. "It's an adorable opportunity.
But I believe I'll pass it up. I intend to spend the afternoon in Aunty's cool parlor, reading magazine stories
about girls who get everything they want. If I feel *very*
venturesome, I'll go out on the veranda."

"Well . . . as long as you're not being self-sacrificing."

"You mean am I choosing the parlor over the barn so
that you can have a clear field with His Elegance? No,
lamb. I *want* the parlor. I couldn't bear anything else
this afternoon. Except maybe another swim. Would you
like to swim? I mean, when you're through sitting on
boards? Besides, I have to think of Brad. I can't go being
second carpenter's assistant to men like Matthew when

Brad is being so faithful in Baltimore. I *believe* it's Baltimore he's being faithful in. Maybe I'll even write him a letter from the parlor. That would be nice of me."

"Especially since he writes to you every day." Jenny was a poor correspondent, but Brad wrote every single day. To write *or* receive a letter from the same person every single day seemed deadly to Miranda.

"I don't know why it is," said Jenny as they went downstairs, "that men in magazine stories always seem so much more attractive than men who are just around. But they usually do."

"The ones in magazines are always putting their best foot forward. Feet forward? You can't expect a real man to be putting his best foot forward all the time. Anyway, a real one lasts longer than a few pages. That's a disadvantage, probably."

I don't believe this, Miranda thought. All this I'm saying is nothing I believe since I met Matthew, who is the sum of everything that's beautiful and wise and is very much a real person. Oh, I am in love at last, she thought in passionate silence. In love, in love . . . Even if in secret, even if almost certainly without hope, being in love was all that mattered.

"Anyway," Jenny was saying, "real men don't even always have a best foot. I've known men whose both feet were hopeless. Women, too," she added fairly. "Hi, Aunty. Can we help with lunch?"

Conversation at the table that afternoon consisted almost entirely of Jenny's explanation of internecine warfare on a women's magazine. There was nothing, but *nothing* as unpredictable, unreliable, exhilarating, stimulating and confounding as publishing, especially magazine publishing.

"You should know about it," she said enthusiastically to Matt. "You've had *stories* published, Aunty says."

"In *Harper's*," he said. "I believe it's somewhat diff—"

"*Harper's Bazaar?*" Jenny interrupted, but with the utmost respect.

"*Harper's Monthly.*"

"Oh. Well, then maybe you wouldn't know, but honestly I could tell you things that would frappé your *blood.*"

"You already have," said Mrs. Long. "I've been sitting here blessing my stars I run a peaceful little boardinghouse. And there *have* been times, mind you, when I thought summer boarders were the most unpleasant people imaginable."

"Oh, I *adore* the magazine," Jenny said. "The craziness is half the *fun.*"

"I'll take my boarders, thank you. More chive tomatoes, anyone?"

When lunch was over, Miranda waited with happy expectancy for a renewal of the invitation (she considered it an invitation) to work in the broiling barn. Matt had disappeared, and while she did the dishes with Jenny she wondered if he could possibly have forgotten. With unusual resolve, she decided that if he had, she'd simply seek him out.

"There," said Jenny, putting away the last dish. "That's that. Are you actually going out in that place? You'll cook."

"Well, I—"

"Miranda?" Matthew was with them again. "How about it? Think you can stand to help me for a while? I warn you, it's going to be hot and sawdusty." He had changed into old paint-stained shorts, a tee shirt and a pair of dirty sneakers. Miranda had never seen anyone so appealing in her life.

"I'd like to," she said. "I don't mind the heat. I *like* it."

"Don't overdo," Jenny muttered, and Miranda flapped a warning hand behind her back.

"You'd better get into something not so nice, then," said Matt. "You're entirely too fine for the sort of work I have in mind."

Miranda flew upstairs. Maybe she *was* overdoing, but it somehow didn't seem to matter. It's only for this weekend, she told herself. I won't ever see him again, so what difference does it make if I seem eager, when I am? After this weekend, she repeated like a lesson, I won't see Matthew again.

It was a lesson that should have hurt, should have been more painful than any other she'd ever learned, but for the moment it seemed no more than words. She did not think anything would change, did not believe that after all when the weekend was past she and he would meet again somewhere, by some chance. Only for now, minutes and hours and these two days were enough. And when the two days of minutes and hours were past and she was back in New York, far from Matthew? She was so in love that it seemed to her just knowing he was alive would be all she needed. Just to be in the same world with him was enough.

Chapter Nine

ONE SIDE of the garage was occupied by the old sedan. On the other side a carpenter's bench, a power saw, cans of paint and turpentine, some sawhorses, an assortment of tools and boards took up most of the space.

"Something short of ship-shape," Matt said apologetically. "I'll even get to cleaning up here one day, I think."

"It's nice," said Miranda. She looked up toward the loft. It seemed to be a storage place for furniture and crates and old garden tools, but once, she supposed, there had been great piles of shining amber hay up there, and horses down here waiting to eat it, stomping their big feet, swishing their coarse tails, whinnying. Where the car was now, a carriage had once stood, no doubt, spindly and pretty, like a carriage on a Christmas card. It's only in the country, she thought, that you get a sense of the olden times. In the city everything is always being torn down and something new built. Or even if you live in an old section, it's drab-old. Not nostalgic, not wistful.

There was a curtain of sun at the open doors, and motes of dust drifted, thick and lazy, in the entrance. Matthew Smith had his sawhorses and boards well toward the back, in the shadow, and the windows were open, but in a few minutes he was running with perspiration. Miranda, brushing lank hair back with her forearm, conceded Jenny a point. She was going to cook.

She sat on the board as directed, but it moved beneath her, and Matt put his large foot on it to steady it further. "You must weigh about twenty pounds," he said, wrinkling his nose against the sawdust. "You'll never be a satisfactory board-sitter until you put on weight."

"I'll overeat," Miranda promised, and he grinned at her.

"Do you like doing this?" she asked him after a while.

"This? Making shelves? Oh, sure. I'd like it better if we had a sudden snow, of course."

"I'm sure Mrs. Long wouldn't *want* to have you work if you were too hot."

"Mrs. Long is everybody's godmother. She goes around asking to be taken advantage of."

That's what Barney says about me, Miranda thought. She tried to see a point of similarity between Jenny's aunt and herself, and found none. Probably there were all kinds of different people who asked to be taken advantage of. It sounded awful, but maybe wasn't so bad. Anyway, she thought with conviction, I'd rather be taken than take people.

"She wouldn't say a thing," Matt was going on, "if I

just knocked off work for the rest of the summer. So naturally I work even harder. This is a thing that sometimes happens to people who ask to be taken advantage of. Evens up the score for them a little, don't you think? Besides, it's going to be hot all summer, and after I get through with the kitchen shelves I'm going to rehang all the doors in the house, and after that I've got about half a dozen other projects. Can't stop for the busy old sun. . . . Hop off, like a good girl, I want to reverse this thing."

Like a good girl, Miranda said to herself. He thinks I'm a child. For a while she let him saw and measure in silence, but as this seemed perfectly acceptable to him— he even started whistling through his teeth, like a man all by himself—she said, "Did you write well this morning?"

For a fleeting second she thought he looked irritated, but he shrugged and answered pleasantly enough, "I can't tell."

"You can't? Why not?"

"I can't even tell you that. Sometimes you write a bit, and while you're at it you feel pretty sure Balzac wouldn't kick. Then you read it over and find you've got the Midas touch in reverse. Everything's lead."

"Gee, that's a shame," Miranda said earnestly. "But I expect it doesn't often happen, or you wouldn't go on writing, would you?"

"Let's say it fails to happen on enough occasions to keep me going. Like that carrot in front of the donkey's nose."

Miranda smiled and pulled her shirt away from her back and was framing another question when he forestalled her.

"Let's try this the other way around," he said. "What do you do? When you aren't on vacation, helping handymen?"

"Oh, I'm a stenographer," she said indifferently. He looked at her, waiting, so she went on. "Lots of times I think about all the interesting things I might have done, but what I *did* do was go to business school. Lots of people do that just because it seems the easiest thing, I guess. I always do the easy thing."

"You do?"

"Oh yes. It isn't a nice thing to know about yourself, but I know it about me."

"Anyway, you have yourself convinced of it."

Miranda thought this was about the same thing. She mused a little, remembering the months in business school. "We used to type to music. In school, I mean."

"Really?"

"Uh-huh. *'Kitten on the Keys'* and the *'Shepherd's Dance,'* things like that. It was fun. Only when I started to work in an office I missed it so much I had to sing to myself. I did that for ages. . . ." He was looking at her in a way that made her feel appealing, an exciting sensation that also made her shy. "Pumfret & Son," she hurried on, too moved to linger over the moment, "is not exactly the sort of place to sing in."

"You don't like it there?"

"I don't not like it, precisely. I mean, I don't see any point in not liking something you have to do—"

"Perhaps there's a point in not doing something you don't like, though. Isn't that reasonable?"

"Reasonable," Miranda echoed. "Well, maybe. But I told you I'm lazy. Pumfret's is underwear," she added. "Men's underwear. Not very interesting."

"I can see where it wouldn't be. What sort of work would you like?"

"But that's the trouble. I never think of what sort of *work* . . . I only think what sort of *office* I could do it in. I wouldn't even mind knit goods so much in Rockefeller Center. I'm not ambitious, like Jenny."

"She does seem to be."

"Jenny's always been very sure of herself." She broke off. "Why do you look like that?"

"Her nails. She may seem sure of herself, but something's wrong or she wouldn't be biting her nails."

"She knows *just* what she wants," Miranda said stubbornly. "Except Brad, maybe. She isn't so sure she wants him." As soon as she'd said it, it sounded indiscreet. Still, Jenny had spoken of Brad at lunchtime. She'd told them she was going to write him a letter, as if saying it would make her do it, and she hadn't sounded enthusiastic.

"Brad's the one she's going to write to if it kills her?" Matt inquired.

"She didn't say that, exactly."

"All but."

"Well, she should write to him. He writes to her every day."

Matt's eyes widened. "Every day? That isn't love, it's persecution."

Miranda started. "You know, that's just what I thought. I mean, I didn't put it like that, but it does seem to me that every day could get to be sort of a burden."

For a while they were silent again. Matt measured and mitered. The sun, falling lower, crept along the barn floor almost to their corner. From time to time something rustled in the loft, creaked in the walls, stirred indefinably. Outside, the sun-drugged cicadas hummed, and far off a crow cawed a warning and a dog barked. Miranda, drowsy and content, followed directions and watched, from secret lids, her love.

Finally she said, "Do you work all the time?" He nodded. "Well, but why?"

"Compulsion, maybe? I don't know."

"Mrs. Long says you're a moving-man, too."

"That's something I certainly am," he said with a grin.

"Writer or handyman, problematical. Moving-man, def."

"Isn't it awfully hard work?"

"You get used to the manual part. I sort of like the rest. Different people, different houses, all sorts of tricky ways to get furniture in and out of places. You'd be surprised, the challenges we face."

"When are you going back to it?"

"Another month, maybe, As a matter of fact, I'm going

in for a couple of days this week and help out with a big
job. Then back here till the book—" His voice trailed
away, and he invited her off the board he'd been working
on and began to measure it against one he'd finished. He
let out a roar of anger and indignation. "Oh, cripes!"

"What's the matter?" she asked anxiously.

"I cut this accursed board shorter than the other one."

Miranda felt tender and solicitous. "That's a shame,
Matt." It was the first time she'd said his name, and it
warmed her happily. "That's just a shame. Isn't there
somewhere else you could use it?"

"Maybe in the basement. It's just so—" He stretched,
wiped his face vigorously. "Listen, let's quit for a while
and take a swim, okay?"

Miranda jumped up. "I'd *love* it," she said, and Matthew Smith burst out laughing. "I don't mean I don't
like helping—" she began, but he said he didn't blame
her in the least. "Meet you at the lake in ten minutes,"
he offered.

Jenny, happy to relinquish the letter she'd barely begun, followed Miranda upstairs and they got into their
bathing suits. Miranda's was still faintly damp from the
morning, but Jenny had another.

"You don't *mind?*" she asked anxiously, twisting and
turning to see herself in the bureau mirror.

"No," said Miranda, who did. "It's gorgeous." She
looked at it a bit apprehensively. Her own was nowhere as
nice, and Jenny did look superb. Matthew Smith . . . Oh,
well, maybe he wouldn't notice. She looked at Jenny

again. Well, then, he'd notice. But maybe he wouldn't care. Maybe, besides, he had that girl somewhere that he was madly in love with and wouldn't care really how anyone else looked. He certainly knows some fascinating people, she thought. Being a writer and all. She had no notion what a writer's life would be like—even a writer who was a moving-man by trade—but it had a glamorous sound, so she peopled it vaguely, and unhappily, with glamorous women.

"I bet he knows some stunning people," she said to Jenny.

"Are you falling for him?"

"You'd hardly fall for someone you've only known a day," Miranda evaded. "I just said I suppose he knows . . . Oh, well." There was no point in repeating it. It only made her sad.

"He's awfully—I mean, frightfully—attractive. Maybe he's writing a best-seller, too. Maybe right this minute a best-seller is being born. Wouldn't that be di*vine?*"

"No," said Miranda in confusion. "I mean, yes. It'd be marvelous. Come on, Jenny. Aren't you ready yet?"

After dinner that evening Mrs. Long said she'd like to go in to town to the movies, if anyone thought that was a good idea. "A revival of *Waterfront*," she explained. "I missed it the first time."

There was a pause, and then Jenny said lazily, "Okay with me. I haven't seen it."

Miranda, a perfectly willing movie-goer in the city, did not like the idea in the country. In her status as a guest, though, she was beginning a reluctant assent when Mrs. Long said, "Don't anyone, *please,* come because I suggested it. That would be too awful. People ought to learn to be more honest with each other, I say. The world would wag along a lot friendlier than it does. This is your vacation, girls, so you do what you want. Matt will, anyway. Do what he wants, that is."

"Well . . ." said Miranda, and then recalled a perfectly good excuse. "For one thing, I've seen it already."

"Good," said Matt. "You can help me take down some doors." He had gone back to the barn to work that day after their swim, and Miranda had so yearned to accompany him that she'd decided she'd better not, and had spent the time—quite happily, it turned out—weeding in the garden with Mrs. Long. Jenny, who felt free to do what she wanted without being told, had read in the cool parlor.

"Now, this girl is not going to work any more," Mrs. Long said to Matt. "She's worked ever since she got here."

"Oh, but I like it," Miranda said anxiously. "Honestly. It's not like work, it's fun."

"See?" said Matt to his hostess. "If I'm to get those doors hung before your guests arrive—I'm assuming they're narrow-minded and will require doors on their rooms—then I'll have to get started tonight. And many hands and so forth—"

"If she wants to," Mrs. Long said firmly.

"Want me to drive you to the movies?" Matt asked. Mrs. Long shook her head. "I'm sure Jenny trusts me to drive, don't you, dear?" she said to her niece.

"Aunty, I'm in your hands."

After they'd gone, Miranda and Matthew Smith sat awhile longer on the shady veranda. It was dusk, and the air rang with birdcalls, thrummed with cricket fiddling. Even as they sat there a sudden rain began to fall in enormous drops that made tiny craters in the dust of the road and fell pattering on the broad flat leaves of the grape arbor growing against the house. It passed in minutes.

"That's funny," Miranda said. "I never saw a rain like that before."

"We get a lot of little freshets of rain in the country," Matt said. "Probably in the city, too, but I guess they're dispersed somewhere in upper air there."

"I guess."

Miranda looked at him, and looked away. She'd thought that when Jenny and Mrs. Long were gone from the house, when she was actually all alone with Matthew Smith, she'd feel pulsy and strange. Instead, she felt peaceful. It was disappointing.

She decided it was Matt's doing. He was so at ease, so loungy and unalert to tremulous feelings. She might have been with Barney. He does have a girl somewhere, she thought. I just know he does. And he treats me like a sister, or a child. "I don't think I'll help you with the doors, after all," she said abruptly.

"Oh?" He sounded surprised, but nothing more. "All right. I don't have to start for a while anyway."

He doesn't even *care*, Miranda protested silently. It doesn't matter to him what I do. She really felt close to tears.

Several minutes passed, Miranda telling herself she wouldn't be the first to speak if they sat here in silence till Jenny and Mrs. Long returned. She shifted to the wicker chair, thought uncomfortably that he could probably hear her swallowing, leaned over to rub her ankle that had begun to itch, and sighed. He apparently wasn't troubled by silences. The way, for instance, John Jr. was. John had to fill every second with nudgings and conversation, and Miranda felt she could understand him better than this man who lay back wordless and unmoving while the minutes passed, and passed.

"When are you going into New York for that job?" she said. The words were out before she knew she was going to speak, and she had again that peculiar sense of understanding John. This was what he did. Blurted. She wondered if it disturbed him as much as it did her. Not to have the mastery of your own tongue? It was awful. . . .

"Wednesday, I guess," Matt was saying. He sat up straighter, glanced at his watch.

"It's a very big job?" she persisted, trying to keep him with her.

"Yup. I probably won't get back here till Friday."

Couldn't I ask him for dinner? Miranda wondered with desperate daring. He'll be tired, working that way, and he lives alone. Couldn't I say, We'd be delighted to give you a nice home-cooked meal—She thought of her mother's reaction, of her mother's cooking, and knew there was no way to make such an invitation anything but what it was, a ruse to see him. And I can't cook a decent meal myself, she thought angrily. What have I been doing or learning all these years? Yet she realized that even if she and her mother had been cookery experts, she would not have been able to ask him, because the invitation would still have appeared to be just what it was.

Girls just have to sit and wait, she thought, helpless and resentful. Sit and wait and hope. He knows I live in the city, he knows I'm going back there. Or he could ask. He could say, Why don't I give you a ring when I'm in? He wasn't going to move furniture every single moment from Wednesday to Friday. He'd have some time free. But not for me, she told herself. He isn't going to have time for me, and he never will have, but I am in love with him, and I will take what I can get, whatever part of his time I can have. So, when he stood and said he'd better get at the doors, she jumped to her feet.

"Where do we start?" she asked.

"I thought you weren't going to."

"I've changed my mind."

Matt stood looking at her for a moment, a smiling, speculative expression in his eyes. "You know," he said, "someday I'm going to write a *Boys' Book of Girls*. It's going to explain to those younger than I—those innocents standing on the rim of girl-consciousness—just what it is they're getting into, and what these creatures are all about."

"Do *you* know?" said Miranda softly.

"Not in the least. That's why I'm going to write it *some*day."

An unaccustomed mischief took possession of her. "No girl-consciousness for you?" she said in the same soft voice.

He looked at her with surprise. "I seem," he said at length, "to be feeling a touch of Miranda-consciousness."

Her breath coming lightly, eyes unwaveringly fixed on his face, Miranda waited, saying silently, repeatedly, *Kiss me, Matt . . . please kiss me.*

The phone rang, and Matt moved to answer it. When he'd explained that Mrs. Long was out and would not be back until around eleven, he hung up and turned back to Miranda, the expression of that moment gone from his eyes. He made no reference, no gesture to show that he was aware of what they had been so close to.

"Going to help me with the doors?" he asked cheerfully.

"No," said Miranda. She didn't care if she sounded as hurt as she was.

"Come on, Miranda," he said. "Help me."

She shook her head in stubborn unhappiness, and suddenly he bent, kissed her lightly on the forehead, straightened and said, "If you change your mind, you'll know where to find me by the racket." He was gone, and in a moment she heard him upstairs, tapping something gently with a hammer and whistling through his teeth, the way a man does who's alone and doesn't mind being.

Chapter Ten

THE CITY, during the first week of Miranda's vacation, was visited by a heat wave that silenced even those most given to asking friends and strangers if it was not hot enough for them. Struck with this molten reality, they grew mute. Over the buildings the sky was a blue-white haze, and sidewalks burned through all but the thickest soles. There was little relief in the shade, little relief at night. In apartments like the Parrishes' the heat seemed to store up from day to day in spite of fans and open windows.

"I wish we could buy an air conditioner," Miranda said to Barney one evening. She wore shorts and her lightest shirt, and she'd gotten out of the shower not fifteen minutes earlier, but she was damp and tickly with perspiration.

It was Thursday, and somewhere in New York City there was Matthew. Where? Doing what? He had been in town since last night, but he hadn't telephoned. She hadn't thought he would, and, knowing he would not, she'd waited for the ring that would bring her his voice. She wondered if there were many people like her—able to believe two completely opposite things at the same time —or if it was some unhappy specialty of her own.

"Wish we could buy an iceberg," Barney said. "I'd put it right here in the middle of the room and I'd get a chisel and hack my way right smack into the center of it and then I'd sit there and freeze. Oh, *man*—"

Mrs. Parrish shifted in her chair, picked up a magazine and let it fall, stared out of the window hopelessly. "It's like a punishment," she said at last. "A punishment."

"But for what, Mama?" said Barney. "What for?"

She wouldn't answer. She wouldn't even let on she heard.

Mr. Parrish, sitting stiffly on a straight chair he'd brought from the kitchen, stretched his thin neck and said, "I gotta good mind not to go to work at all tonight. Cab's like a hot box, and that lousy muffler, they never fixed it yet."

"Pop, why don't you tell them you won't *drive* unless they fix it?" Miranda asked. "Just tell them."

"I'm gonna have a settee with the boss about it, all right." He got to his feet, looked around for his cap and put it on.

"Thought you weren't going," Barney said lazily. "And it's set-to, not settee."

"I said what I hadda mind not to, not what I was gonna. Since when's my mind got anythin' to do with the price a things? And stop correctin' my English."

"Your what?" Barney muttered.

"You bring in some milk in the morning, okay?" said Mrs. Parrish, hardly moving her lips. "We need some milk."

"If I remember," said her husband.

"Well, remember. You're the one wants milk in your coffee."

Mr. Parrish went, and there was silence, and then Barney got up as though it hurt him and moved over to the television set.

Mrs. Parrish brightened. "No date tonight?" she said to her son.

"Not on your life. I'm going to die right here at home, not out on a sizzling sidewalk with no one but strangers to see me over the river." There was a roar of studio laughter, and Barney stared sourly at a tattersall-vested comedian.

"Oh, leave him on," said Mrs. Parrish. Barney looked briefly argumentative and then gave in.

I wonder if Jenny would want to go to a movie, Miranda thought. At least they're cool. On the other hand, you had to get to them and return, which was too much to think of. Besides, she wasn't sure she wanted to see Jenny just yet. They'd parted at the bus stop four days ago and hadn't met since, though Jenny had called once to report blissfully that the fashion editor had asked for her as a replacement, "while her own secretary's on vacation, Miranda, and who knows what may come of *this.* . . ." She'd gone on for a while, not once mentioning the heat, and not mentioning, either, the weekend past. Well, naturally, Miranda had thought. Naturally. The weekend's over, as far as Jenny's concerned. Over, and never very important anyway.

On the bus coming home she'd said that Miranda had been awfully quiet all day Sunday. "Were you getting bored, or something? I *told* you there isn't much to do in the country. For my part, I love *Aunty,* but I'm glad to be getting back where the chickens aren't. Like the pigeon and the cockroach, I'm urban. What did you think of that Matt, disappearing that way. I'd certainly hate to be a writer if I had to hole up like that all the time, *work*ing."

"How are you going to be an editor, then?"

"That's different, Miranda," Jenny said, not explaining how. "Besides, it wasn't awfully *polite* of him. I hope you didn't mind, Miranda. I mean, you weren't fond of him, or anything, were you?"

Yesterday, Miranda thought, she was accusing me of being in love with him. "No. I mean I like him well enough, but I didn't care—" she swallowed painfully "—didn't mind about not seeing him today. After all, a man's work . . ." She trailed into silence.

"Still, I expect it was rude. After being so friendly and all, yesterday. Men are funny," said Jenny with happy indifference.

"Aren't they just."

Miranda had written a thank-you note to Mrs. Long, and, after a nervous, lengthy debate with herself, had added a postscript saying to remember her to Matthew

Smith. She'd spelled his name out like that, very formally.

And she couldn't stop remembering him, couldn't stop thinking of the afternoon in the barn, of the lovely conversations they'd had, of the evening when they'd been alone.

Why had he kissed her on the forehead? To be friendly? To be kind? Because he was sorry for something and didn't wish to say so? She could not help knowing it was the kiss of an adult to a hurt child that must bear the hurt and cannot be really comforted. A kindly adult would do that, as a gesture. Only—for a moment, before the phone rang—he had not been looking at her the way a grown-up looks at a child. He had been a man looking at a woman. *I seem to be feeling a touch of Miranda-consciousness,* he'd said, and her being had lifted to the sound in his voice. I never wanted anything so much in my life, she thought now, as I wanted Matt to kiss me then, that moment, and I probably never will want anything that much again.

Oh, but that's silly, she told herself crossly. He isn't the only man in the world, and I'll want something from some other man just as much someday. There'll be another man like Matt somewhere.

"Mama," Barney said protestingly. "I cannot stand this jerk."

"Find something else!" Mrs. Parrish flared. She wiped her forehead with a man's handkerchief, pulled her dress away from her neck and threw a baited look around the room, as though searching for a way out of the heat.

"Where are you going, Miranda?"

"To my room," Miranda said, faltering at the door. "Why, Mama? Is there something you want?"

Mrs. Parrish didn't think there was. She explained that even if she did think so, who was going to do anything for her anyway. She did think it was a shame, the way they never stayed together or acted like they wanted to or were a family at all. Barney getting mad about the television, and who turned it on in the first place . . . Miranda stamping off to her room, and who was to blame? That was what she'd like to know. Who was to blame?

"I wasn't stamping," Miranda said.

"To blame for what?" Barney asked, snapping off the television set.

"For how we ain't like a family," said Mrs. Parrish. "For how your father is gone every night, and so are you, mostly, and Miranda off in her room if she isn't out, and me left here alone all the time."

"As a matter of fact," Barney pointed out, "you aren't. Most of the time you're out visiting, or downstairs on the sidewalk with your chair and the neighbors. I bet the only reason you're not down there tonight is it's too hot. *Plenty* of nights I'm here by myself, and once in a while you've got to be by yourself, too. Gluing people together in a room doesn't make a family."

"Then what does, I'd like to know?"

"Search me. Common interests, maybe."

"And we ain't got those, I suppose?"

"Not that I know of," said Barney. "Common needs,

okay. But no common interests. Do you care where the Cardinals stand? Do I give a hang what Mrs. Killjoy has to say about her latest grandchild? Does Miranda pine to know what I'm going to study in college? Does—"

"Miranda's very proud of you going to college," Mrs. Parrish interrupted hotly. "And so are your parents, if you want to know."

Barney grimaced. "Mama, I didn't say we weren't interested in each other. I said we don't have common interests, which is a different matter. And we don't. And, furthermore, I'll bet you couldn't point out to me *one* family that behaves like whatever it is you think a family should behave like."

Mrs. Parrish slumped in her chair, as if the small interchange had exhausted her. "I wish life was easier," she said. "I wish it was nicer, and easier."

"So do I," said Barney. "I guess we all wish that."

Miranda was still at the door, wanting to get away, unsure if she should leave or come back into the room and try to act like a family. Poor Mama. It was hard on her. Except you couldn't help remembering that she usually only wanted them to be together when she happened to be home herself. Miranda doubted very much if her mother would stay in for a spot of togetherness if she happened to have a canasta date on, and Barney wasn't the only one who spent evenings alone in this apartment.

And the trouble was, when they were together this sort of thing happened. Well, not all the time. But too often they ended up with each of them marooned in a separate silence. Here they were, the living room growing dark, the shabby furniture melting into shadows, her mother an indistinguishable bulk in her chair near the window, Barney a long shape on the floor, and herself in the doorway, probably no longer heeded, but not sure.

"Shall I turn on a light?" she asked.

"No," said her mother. "It's too hot. Barney, see can you find something else on the television, willya?"

Miranda fled down the hall to her room.

I want someone, she thought, lying on her bed, staring into the shadows. She reached over and turned on her lamp. I want someone to understand me, someone that I can understand, someone that I'd want to be together with, always.

A few hot tears gathered at the corners of her eyes and streaked down her face to the pillow. She brushed them away, and no more came. She didn't feel like crying. There was nothing to cry about. If you cried because you felt alone, you'd be crying too much, and besides—she just didn't feel like it.

I feel something, she thought, but it isn't a need for tears. It wasn't just his kiss I wanted. I have never been with any other person that I liked talking to, listening to, *being* with so much.

This is Thursday, and Matthew is in town, and he will never think to call me.

There was a feather on her pillow. She noticed it when she turned her head idly, and lay for a while looking at it. Then she sat up, holding it in her fingers, and threw it.

It drifted a couple of inches upward and spiraled back onto her lap. She picked it up and tried a few times again to throw it from her, but it never went far. It hung lazily in air and then fell, but it would not go away. Feeling silly, sentimental and really unhappy, she tossed the feather away and watched it come back.

Why did he seem to like me, and then, when I had only that one day left, stay in his room and work all the time and only come out for dinner and to drive us to the bus?

After he'd gone upstairs that evening, she remained in stiff silence on the veranda for perhaps half an hour, waiting for him to come back and ask for her help once again. Waiting for him at least to call down and ask what she was doing. And nothing happened. He went on working somewhere upstairs, and she sat listening to the crickets until she could not bear it any more. She stood and took a couple of deep breaths and went to him.

"Matt?" she said quietly, stopping at the head of the stairs and looking toward him down the hall. "Matt? Could I help?"

He had a door on the floor and was tapping some hinges or something into place. "Hi, Miranda. Actually, there's nothing you can do."

"But—" she said in a faint voice "—but before, you said there was."

He smiled slightly, pulled a pencil from behind his ear and made a mark on the door frame. "Oh, that was probably just an excuse. To get your company, you know."

A girl could have found the words beautiful if she hadn't listened to the tone of the voice. Listening, Miranda found no welcome. She sat on the floor, a little distance away from him, and watched, and heard his polite comments, and wondered what had happened. You can't *ask* people, she thought. You can't say, "Please, Matt . . . why did you like me, because you *did* like me, and then suddenly not want me around you at all?" He wasn't the same man that she'd laughed with in the hot afternoon sun, and he wasn't the same man who had looked at her as a woman and kissed her as a child in the hall just a little while ago. This was someone who was too courteously putting up with her presence, and here she sat, being put up with because she could not make herself leave.

Chilled, unhappy, without an answer, she stayed with him until Jenny and her aunt came home. She hadn't seen him the next day until dinnertime.

"I thought he was going to get all those *doors* hung," Jenny said to Mrs. Long as the three of them gathered currants in the garden on Sunday.

"I suppose he's inspired," Mrs. Long said. "He's got this chapter plotted and has to get it all written. Before it slinks out of his head, I guess. Writers are like that."

"Maybe," said Jenny. "Only what about the doors?"

"He'll get them done, dearie. Never you fear. Miranda, look at the butterfly just in back of you . . . isn't he a beauty?"

In no mood for butterflies, Miranda looked and said yes, it was a beauty.

Twirling the feather, Miranda sat in her room, remembering. She suddenly turned and looked toward the window. A gust of air—you couldn't call it a breeze—moved through the massy air of the room. At the same time there was a short, sluggish sound of thunder in the distance. She walked to the window and leaned out, turning her head up to see if there were hopeful signs. It was too dark to tell, but as she stood there, the sky was vividly and tremendously lit. The roofs of buildings opposite, whiskered with aerials, appeared in a brief, sharp cut-out, and everything was blacker than before. Thunder again, closer, louder, angrier, and a freshened, acrid odor in the air. Then the rain came, straight and heavy. Miranda held her hand near the screen, but it was spattering in only lightly. She left the window open and stood, breathing deeply and looking down at the sidewalks, deserted and already steaming wet in the light of the street lamps. She still held the feather.

Oh, well, she thought, and slid the screen open a little. She thrust her hand out in the drowning night, and the feather was taken from her fingers in an instant.

You could go just so far with melodrama, and repine just so far. She had seen, from a merry-go-round, a man she might have loved. She had met, at a lake, a man who was like him, and she fell in love. But Jenny, if she knew about it, would say she was in love with love, and maybe Jenny was right.

With love or with Matthew, she thought, it's awfully real, and I can't stop feeling it. But I'll get used to it. And sometime—oh, surely sometime—another young man will be enough like Matthew, enough like the boy in Palisades Park, to make me forget them and love him.

Miranda was far too young and healthy to dedicate herself forever to something not only lost but never really possessed.

Testing once again to be sure she could leave the window open, she went back to the living room. They'd turned the lights on, the television off, and were sitting quietly, giving their grateful attention to the downpour of night rain.

"I have an idea," Miranda said. "Why don't we play canasta?"

"Okay by me," Barney said, and Mrs. Parrish said she'd love it.

Two or three times during the next couple of hours, as they slapped down their cards and argued amiably and heard the rain dwindle and stop and leave them in an air that could almost be called cool, Mrs. Parrish looked from one to the other of her children and said, "This is what I call nice. Sitting here playing cards together this way. I call it real nice."

We're a family, Miranda thought. Even if we don't always know it, or even always want it, we are a family.

Chapter Eleven

"Now, that's a funny thing," said Mrs. Parrish, coming into Miranda's room to waken her one morning the following week. "Wake up, honey."

"I'm awake, Mama."

"Can't get used to you laying in bed this way," said Mrs. Parrish with good-humored sarcasm.

"Nothing else to do," Miranda answered indifferently.

"I guess you ain't had much fun on your vacation, except your weekend away that you won't even talk about. Least, I hope you had fun then."

"It's been all right. I get to sleep as late as I want to, don't I?" Then she laughed. "As Barney says, it's better to have half a loaf than never to have loafed at all."

"Oh, for goodness sakes, here we are talking away and there's a call for you. That's what I was saying was funny—"

"Call? You mean someone's waiting on the phone? Oh, Mama, really—" Miranda threw back the sheets and started out of the room.

"It's that Mr. Pumfret," Mrs. Parrish called after her. "I hope nothing's gone wrong. They ain't gonna fire you, or—"

"Hello?" said Miranda. "Mr. Pumfret? I'm sorry to have kept you waiting—"

"Miss Parrish? This is John Pumfret." Pause, and then, "Junior."

"Yes. Yes, I recognize your voice, Mr. Pumfret." Another pause. "How are you?"

"I'm well, thank you. How are you?"

"I'm fine," said Miranda, polite and mystified.

"Did you have a good time that weekend?"

"It was very nice." Pause again, and she said, feeling slightly crazy, "Have you been having a good time?"

"Yes. No. That is, who can tell?"

Having no answer to that, she waited, and then when he didn't speak, said, hoping to discover what this was all about, "It's nice to hear from you." She might better have said peculiar, but just the same—

"I'm glad you said that. Because, you see, I was wondering if you would go to the museum with me today. I decided to run in, and then remembered how much you enjoy it, so I thought that perhaps . . . not if you're busy, naturally."

"I'm not busy," Miranda said slowly.

"Well, then, if you'd like to—"

"I'd like it very much."

She wasn't sure she meant that, but she didn't have anything else to do, and as usual found it hard to refuse a direct invitation. Besides, it was too odd an invitation to refuse. She would not admit to herself that she didn't have the resolution to say no to the boss's son. This perception entered her mind and was promptly driven out by pride.

He said that he would be on the museum steps in, say, an hour? Miranda agreed and hung up and the phone rang again instantly.

"Miranda, how are you? I'm in my office . . . get the *my* . . . and this is my *first* personal phone call on company time, which I am perfectly free to do this week and I thought I'd make it to you."

"I'm flattered. How's the new job?"

"Oh, it's divine and I'm going to *perish* when they throw me back in the pool."

"Maybe they won't."

A sigh from Jenny. "Not a chance of staying here, I'm afraid. But at least they're more and more *aware* of me now. And Miss Vandroff, the fashion editor, you know, is darling to me. Honestly, I don't think it was a bad idea at *all* that I made such a mess of my hair. I stick *out* so. What're you doing?"

"Believe it or not, I'm off to the museum to prowl around armor some more with John R. Pumfret, Jr."

"No!" Jenny shrieked. "How simply dashing for you."

"He called up and said would I, and I said I would, and I'm going to meet him on the museum steps in an hour. Which means I better hang up now."

"Meet him? Where is he?" Jenny asked sharply.

"Jenny, he's in Scarsdale."

"Look, does this person *know* where you live?"

"I don't think so."

"Well, he could ask. Miranda, you make him drive you *home*, hear? I am not asking, I'm *telling* you. Either he drives you home, or you have *nothing* more to do with him. . . ."

Miranda smiled, and tried not to let the smile get into her voice. "We'll see."

"Don't we'll see me, Miranda. If he called you, he's interested, and the only way to keep him interested is to *value* yourself, and if he doesn't drive you home, the next time he asks you to go mucking around in that morgue, you just say sorry, but I'm previously engaged for the rest of my *life*. I've told you, Miranda, *nothing* succeeds like the cold shoulder—"

"Yes, teacher," Miranda said meekly. "Of course, I won't even be there to give him a cold shoulder if you don't let me off the phone."

"Oh, sure. Well, toodle-oo. Now remember what I *said*."

Miranda turned away from the phone laughing, and Mrs. Parrish said, "That Jenny? I wish *I* could put you in a good mood, the way some of your friends do—"

"Mama, Mr. Pumfret, Jr., wants me to go to the museum with him."

"He does?" Mrs. Parish looked blank. "Is he fast?"

"Oh, Mama. He's the slowest thing on feet. I guess," she added, realizing that she didn't actually know. "Why do you ask that?"

"Well, the boss's son. A girl's gotta be careful."

"Mama, dear," Miranda said fondly. "That's sort of old-fashioned, isn't it?"

"Some things are never old-fashioned. How do you know he ain't a . . . a rascal?"

"He isn't a rascally type, that's all. I went out with him once before, anyway. To the museum that time, too. I don't think rascals go to museums."

"You did? You didn't tell me."

"I told Pop."

"That's right. Tell your father everything, but your mother—"

"I didn't think it was very important, Mama. Probably I just plain forgot. I better get dressed."

"How could you forget you'd gone out with the boss's son?"

"Just the same, I must have. Mama, I *have* to get dressed."

"You want some breakfast?" Mrs. Parrish offered unexpectedly, as though Miranda were going into possible peril and might need to be fortified.

"Coffee and fruit juice is enough. That'd be nice, Mama."

"Why would the boss's son ask you out, is what I want to know. I'm not sure I like it."

"He's a perfectly harmless young man. Sort of sad, really."

"Sad? With all his money?"

"They don't have such a lot of money, Mama. I've told you that. To hear them talk, you'd think they underwrote

134

Rockefeller, but Mr. Pumfret is just a small business-man."

"Putting on airs, when they just make beans," said Mrs. Parrish in easy reversal.

Miranda laughed and gave up. She went to her room to dress, not thinking much about the afternoon ahead of her because she didn't know what to think of it. Without feeling in the least unworthy, she still found it odd that John Jr. should ask her out.

This time they did not stay in the museum long. They went briefly into a wing they hadn't visited on the last trip, to see Oriental armor, lighter and wilder-looking than that of Europe, and every bit as damascened, etched, embossed, gilded and bejeweled. Almost too nice for fighting in, Miranda thought. They went to see the Earl of Cumberland's armor, which was John's favorite, and he explained, as he had before, that the decorations on the Earl's colorful suit, the cinquefoil roses, the fleurs-de-lis connected by true-lovers' knots, were emblems of the House of Tudor. "The cipher of Queen Elizabeth—Elizabeth I, of course—was gilded or etched on every element of Cumberland's harness. He was the Queen's personal protector, you know. A glorious example of knighthood. The prototype of chivalry." John's voice was ardent.

Miranda suppressed a yawn.

Yet, for all his guidebook talk and his genuine interest, it was a bare half-hour before he looked at his watch and asked if she was ready for lunch. "All right," she said with surprise, and, thinking of Jenny, wished she had the nerve to suggest the Plaza. She did not, and they went to the museum cafeteria once again.

John selected a fairly isolated table, quickly disposed of his food, leaned forward a little and, in a low voice, began to talk. Listening in a state of shock, pity and irritation, Miranda said to herself that this was more like an attack than a conversation. She didn't know what to say, but wouldn't have had a chance to say it anyway. He was like a torrent rushing through a burst dam, and he clearly wanted her attention, not her opinion.

He started pretty far back, with a boarding school, the aim of which had been to make John wretched. From there he went to fraternity brothers who had let him down, girls who had turned out to be interested in no one but themselves (that *would* be a let-down, Miranda thought, wondering if her helpless silence was being interpreted as interest in him, and deciding it probably was), the work he had wanted to do and was prevented from doing by his father (he was not clear what the wished-for work would have been), and, finally, his mother's attitude toward him.

Now we're coming to the home stretch, Miranda said to herself. It's the mothers who catch it, the mothers who cap all the indignities and injustices, who are to blame, apparently, for everything. It was enough to make a girl wonder if she'd ever have the courage to be one, knowing all the faults and failures that were going to be laid at her feet when the children began to grow up. It might be

better never to marry and take up baby nursing as a pro-
fession. That way you'd get to be with the babies, the only
people in the world who take other people as they are,
but you'd avoid the . . . odium was probably the word,
of bringing them up.

". . . I don't know what your mother is like," John was
saying, not in the least interested in what Miranda's
mother was like, "but mine's a seismograph. If I were at
the other end of the world and had a tremor of an idea,
it'd register on my mother and she'd send out the marines
to stop me, and the thing is, I'd be stopped. Where are you
going, Junior? What are you thinking about? Is that an
idea you have, Junior, or are you just making faces?
Where's your handkerchief, your vitamin pill, your sense,
your spirit, Junior? Bring your spirit out here in the
light where Mother can examine it, Junior. . . ."

He stopped, breathless for a moment, and charged on.
Miranda studied the figures in the pool, greeny metal
water sprites with thin bodies and odd unpleasant faces;
they balanced on their toes and held fountains in their
upstretched hands. The sound of splashing water was
lovely and she tried to listen to it instead of John. And
it's perfectly possible, she thought, that after this outburst
he won't ever want to see or talk to me again. Often it
works out that way, and it wouldn't make things exactly
cozy around the office. Oh, dear . . .

John gave a forced laugh and leaned forward, his cheeks
burning. With his face so close, Miranda had an uneasy
and resentful sensation of being victimized. There wasn't

a thing she could do except listen. But that mild, fatuous John should suddenly appear so violent was almost frightening.

"I'm going to tell you something that I've never told anyone before," he said tensely.

"Maybe you'd better not?" she said in a tentative voice, without hope.

"I don't have any friends. Real ones. Not a single one." He sat back, looking triumphant. "And you would like to know why?" Miranda shook her head, but imperceptibly. "Because Mother *pals* with guys I bring around the house. And girls . . . my mother can shrivel a girl in one second flat without opening her mouth. Do you think people are going to put up with that?"

"Why do you?" Miranda said weakly.

"Why, indeed?" he said, sounding spent. "Indeed . . . why? I don't know. May I call you Miranda?" She nodded silently. "Miranda, then . . . it's a nice name. The only Miranda I ever heard of was the girl in *The Tempest,* the one who'd never seen a man. Are you like that?"

Practically, Miranda thought. And, then, I've seen the one I want. But she didn't intend to say that to John. She never spoke of Matthew, even to Jenny, and she could no more mention him to John than she could . . . well, offer him *any* confidence. With some men you might be able to, but not with John. It didn't matter, of course. John didn't wish to exchange confidences, he only wished to make them. Again she wondered what would happen if he had a sudden revulsion after all this indiscretion. It would certainly be outrageous if she had to leave her job because he couldn't hold his tongue.

And yet, in some indefinable way, his utter, shameless unhappiness seemed, for the moment anyway, to put his needs and claims first. After all, Miranda thought, I have a pretty nice life. Not exciting, and there never do seem to be any challenges to meet, but my family loves me and I have friends, and most of the time I'm really pretty happy. When you had all that, could you say to another human being, I don't want to be bothered with your misery, it bores and disturbs me, and I think your troubles are all your own fault? Even if they were his own fault, and even if the consequences of his outburst were oppressing, didn't you have to listen to someone so completely sad and desperate?

"Can I drop you somewhere?" he asked when they were, finally, out on the street again. His voice sounded damp and worn out. Miranda didn't think that surprising.

"The subway will be all right."

He nodded, and then said, "Where do you live?"

"Washington Heights."

"Where's that?"

"Uptown, on the west side."

"Then I can drop you."

She realized, with faint amusement, that he probably wouldn't have suggested it if she'd lived somewhat out of the way. He's very unhappy, she thought, but he's also unthoughtful and ungenerous. Oh, well . . . maybe that was what happened to unhappy people.

"That would be fine," she said. Actually, she didn't care at all.

But John, having found a good listener, had no intention of releasing her, and this turned out to be just the first in a series of dates. Miranda went back to her job, summer trailed away to make room for fall, and two or three times a week John and Miranda went out together.

"Well, but what do you *do* with him?" Jenny asked persistently. "Do you have any fun?"

Fun, Miranda thought. A word that had no connection with John and his painful, selfish emotions. "We have interesting times," she said slowly. This, to some extent, was true. She was learning things from John besides the art of sympathetic listening, which she'd already had but never before exercised so unremittingly.

"I suppose that's almost as good," Jenny said dubiously. "Except you'd think a person could be interesting *and* fun. At least, you'd hope he could."

I didn't say John was interesting, Miranda thought. I said we did interesting things. It seemed rather disloyal to say this, even to Jenny. "I like the concerts. And the auctions of antiques, and the museums. He does like something besides armor, which is a help. Old masters and old music and old furniture."

"*Every*thing old?"

"Just about." He's aging me, too, she thought. "John was born out of his time. He should have lived in the eighteenth century."

"You've said that before, and I expect it's something he told you. It sounds tremendously dull, but you know what you're doing. I don't think."

Do I? Miranda wondered. I'm spending a lot of time with a discontented young man who hasn't let his family know he's dating me because he says he wants to have something to himself. That it makes me feel sneaky doesn't seem to bother him at all. In the office they all but ignored each other and then, when they had a date, would leave separately and meet a few blocks away. Miranda wondered how long she'd be able to keep it up, no matter how John pleaded. She didn't like Mr. Pumfret, but deceiving him was another matter. John swore it was privacy, not trickery, and so far she'd let herself be persuaded because he always managed to make his needs seem more important than her own.

On the other hand, she'd insisted that John meet her family, and he'd been to the apartment a few times, with discouraging results. As she told Jenny, "John gets on the highest horse you ever saw, Pop gets to be a positive spokesman for the lower classes, and Barney just glares."

"What about your mother?"

"Oh, she's the worst of all. She just plain doesn't like him. She says maybe he'd be all right if he got over everything that was wrong with him and probably there's hope for everyone but she doesn't think so in his case. It's awful."

"I agree with her."

"Oh, come off it, Jenny. You've never even met him."

"I don't have to meet him to know him. He's a type. He's spoiled and selfish and I think he's got years to go before he really cares about anyone but himself, and maybe he'll *never* make it. *You* can hardly stick up for your rights, as it is. A man like that would just ride all over you."

Irritated because she more than half agreed, Miranda said she'd have to work it out for herself.

"Work out *what?*" Jenny demanded, and Miranda thought, with a sort of muffled irony, that John wasn't the only person who rode all over her. Practically the only person she knew who didn't was her father, and he simply wasn't interested in overriding anybody. Unlike John, who also felt overpowered by people, Miranda blamed herself and not them. The trouble, she thought, is that I *put* myself in this position. If you're as wavering and uncertain as I always am, you're just asking to be bullied. Well, perhaps bullied wasn't the word. You were asking, certainly, to be directed and instructed, and if you never stopped people from doing it, naturally they did it more.

I am always, she reproached herself, wondering why life doesn't have any challenges, but isn't this one? And why don't I meet it? Why don't I just stand up and say, politely but firmly, "Allow me, please, to make up my own mind about things." Why don't I tell John I'd rather not see him, Mr. Pumfret I don't want his job, and Mama and Barney that I'm tired of having my character and my friends criticized? Why don't I tell Jenny, right this minute, that there *is* something to work out with

John, and that I want to do it without explaining myself to her?

"I do wish," Jenny was going on, "that you'd meet a nice healthy man who's heard of the twentieth century."

"And I wish," Miranda burst out, "that you'd meet one who was in town more than ten minutes every two months, and where does that leave us?"

Jenny looked at her in astonishment. "Well, for goodness sakes, Miranda. I was only saying it for your own good. Besides, I know what I'm doing with Brad."

Miranda wanted to say that she knew what she was doing with John, but she didn't know, so she couldn't. Besides, she thought impatiently, flaring up at people who really care for me isn't meeting a challenge. There *must* be a way. I just haven't found it yet.

"I'm only saying," Jenny pointed out in a reproving voice, "that we'll have to get you introduced somehow to somebody perfectly lovely. A girl like you, going out with a man who even won't admit he *is* going out with you, that it's all a trick of the light, or something—I ask you, Miranda, what sort of a future is that?"

"I hardly think John's my future."

"Well, but what is? You're nineteen. You're going to have to get started on your future sometime soon, or it'll be past."

"What about your own?" Miranda asked sulkily.

"Oh, lordy. I've been so busy bossing you around," Jenny said in such a disarming way that Miranda no longer felt bossed, "that I forgot to tell you the beautiful

news. The fashion editor's secretary is leaving. For *good.*
She got married, and her husband is making noises about
having her home in a cottage apron and stuff. So . . . *I*
get the job."

"Oh, Jenny!"

"You know how in comics they say someone jumped for
joy? That's what I did. I actually went right up in the air
when they told me."

"Well, it's the nicest news I've heard in ages." They
contemplated Jenny's future with pleasure for a few
moments, and then Miranda asked if Brad had been told.

"Oh, well, Brad," Jenny said uncomfortably. "Not yet.
I'll probably write him tonight. But you know how he is
about me and work. Poisonous. If you ask me, *he* should
be living in the eighteenth century. I asked him once if he
approved of woman suffrage."

Miranda laughed. "What did he say?"

"That he wished he'd been there to put a stop to it.
Then he tried to pretend *that* was facetious. But he
doesn't fool me. Listen, Miranda, when the spring term
starts, you really ought to take this art appreciation
course."

"I told you how I felt about that."

"No, but listen . . . In the first place, it's interesting.
In the second place, there really are a stimulating number
of young men taking it. And they can't *all* be married."

"*Jenny!* I'm not going to go *hunting* men."

"Now, now. You don't have to admit that's what it is.
Don't even admit it to yourself, if you'd rather not. But

just for one clear-eyed second, dearie, face the fact that we *all* do. You don't have to get frantic, and you certainly don't have to go *bargain* hunting, but if a girl wants to fall in love and get married—which you do—then she has to go where the men are. That just stands to reason."

Miranda didn't reply for a while, and then she began diffidently, "Jenny, do you . . . I mean, does your aunt —when she writes, I mean—ever mention Matthew Smith?"

"Oh. Oh, so that's it. I'm surprised that I'm the least surprised."

"You can hardly say that's it that way, since I'll probably never see him again. I just wondered."

"You give up too easily."

"I just see what there is to see, and that's nothing. He knows I live in the city, and he must have been back for weeks now. Or are you suggesting I should call him?"

"No. But, still, something might work out," Jenny said vaguely. "I can't think what, but if a girl likes a man as much as I guess you like him, you'd think Fate would bring them together."

"I guess Fate only works for people who believe in it. *Does* your aunt ever talk about him?"

"She mentioned he'd gone back to his job with the furniture movers and he's working on his novel nights. Probably he's awfully *busy*, Miranda. You know, I did get the distinct feeling that he was sort of drawn to you, that weekend. I don't know why I got it, but I did. I mean, even after he holed up that day and never showed till we were ready to leave. Looked at in one way, it *could* mean that he was so interested he got defensive. Maybe he doesn't think he can write the great American novel and fall in love, too."

"You're building a very pretty brick without a shred of straw."

"Well?" said Jenny. "Isn't there a shred? No sign of a straw that evening Aunty and I were at the movies?"

Miranda hesitated. She found the wish to talk of Matthew stronger than the need to be silent about him. "Well, then, I'll tell you. Yes, sort of a wispy little shred, and it blew away when the phone rang and never blew back again. I think . . . maybe he was going to kiss me. Only he didn't, and he's never done a thing about me since. So wouldn't you say that was that? Besides," she went on with difficulty, "it's peculiar, but I'm not even sure it *is* Matthew I . . . care about. It's—this is awfully hard to explain—it's that I think there's a *type* of man I get attracted to, and he's the type."

"You mean you think there are lots like him?"

"Oh, no," Miranda said indignantly. "Only . . . maybe just one more? That I could meet?"

"I'd say it was remarkable you even met one. I bet loads of people go through life *never* meeting their type. Like me, for instance."

"Well, what about getting married, then?"

"You marry the type that comes along, I suppose. And tell yourself it's what you wanted all along."

"I'll tell *you* something," Miranda said abruptly.

"You'd better think carefully before you marry Brad." She stopped, astonished at having spoken so directly, and quite dismayed. There were too many friendships risked by helpful personal remarks. "Sorry, Jenny—"

"Don't be sorry," Jenny said. "I think people should tell their friends things—I mean, if they really like them, and have their *in*terests at heart. I always think that you're *too* discreet, Miranda. If I didn't know you better, sometimes I'd think it was lack of interest."

"Well, it certainly isn't that. It's just . . . oh, that I never think I know what's good for me, much less what would be good for someone else."

"Maybe you know more than you think," Jenny said thoughtfully.

After a while they went on to talk of other things, and somehow the conversation never did get back, that day, to either Matthew or Brad.

Chapter Twelve

ONE MORNING when Mr. Pumfret was busy on his phone, John Jr. made for the files beside Miranda's desk and, his fingers busily and pointlessly flipping cards, said in a low voice from the side of his mouth, "Tonight, okay? See you at the usual place."

This is awful, Miranda thought, wanting to laugh. We sound like spies. I should write my answer in invisible ink on the top of an invoice and accidentally drop it in his wastebasket. For the first time since their first date, she shook her head.

John so far forgot himself as to say "What?" in his normal voice. Quickly he lowered it to a hoarse carrying whisper. "Why not?"

"I just can't," Miranda whispered back, staring straight ahead and typing steadily.

"But why not? You can't just say no without giving me a reason." He forgot to consult the files and even turned part way toward her.

Miranda, who also felt she couldn't say no without

giving a reason, suddenly rebelled. Why shouldn't she just say no? People did it all the time. They preferred not to do something and they said no, thank you, and they didn't feel obliged to follow it up with explanations about how there was sickness in the family, a relative just in from Detroit, and a possible snowstorm on the way. They just said no.

"No, thank you," said Miranda and went on typing.

"*Listen,*" said John, leaning over her desk. "You can't—" He straightened, lunged at the files and said, "Oh, yes, Dad? You called me?"

Mr. Pumfret, at the door of his office, scowled. "Yes, I called you. Are you dictating?"

"No, no. Just . . . ah, suggesting a change in one of my letters."

"Well, then, come in here. Please."

John hurried in. Miranda flipped a page of her notebook and went on typing, feeling oddly elated.

Half an hour later Mr. Pumfret put on his hat and coat, said he'd be gone for the rest of the day, advised Miranda to be sure to lock up when she left, and departed. John, the minute the door closed, rushed out of hiding and then rushed back again as Mr. Camp came bouncing in.

"Hi, Pumfret," he said to John's disappearing back. "Miranda, how *are* you?" He'd been away for a few days, and getting back to the city always had this cheery effect on him. He put his sample case down, looked around the office as though for changes and then said, "Could you take a few letters, Miranda? Not much."

"Of course, Mr. Camp."

They settled down to work, Mr. Camp with a glad air, and Miranda thankful he'd appeared when he did. At the end of one of his letters Mr. Camp lowered his voice and said, "Miranda?"

I'm beginning to feel like a shameful secret, Miranda said to herself, and wondered what it would be like to have someone yell at the top of his voice, "Hey, Miranda! How about a date?"

"Yes, Mr. Camp."

"*Can't* you call me Charlie?" His whisper was pained.

"No, Mr. Camp. I'm sorry."

He sighed. "And I suppose you can't have lunch with me, either?"

"No, thank you, Mr. Camp." No excuses for him, either. And no more "sorries." Just thanks, no. It was really quite exhilarating.

He resumed dictation.

If I didn't know the situation, Miranda thought, I'd feel sought-after. Two men in one office is a pretty good percentage when there are only four altogether. She decided that probably you only felt sought-after if you enjoyed the seekers.

At lunchtime John steamed through the office as if he were on tracks and disappeared without a word.

"What's eating him?" Mr. Camp asked.

"I don't know," Miranda said shortly. "I didn't get the last sentence, Mr. Camp."

"Ah . . . oh, yes, here we are—"

Fifteen minutes later he rose, asked Miranda if she was sure she wouldn't change her mind, nodded without surprise at her negative and went bouncing off. Not too cast down, Miranda decided, and forgot him.

She went to the washroom to tidy up, and found Connie fluffing her hair before the mirror.

"Gotta lunch date?" Connie inquired brightly. Miranda shook her head. "Oh, good. Let's go over to that tearoom, then, huh?"

"Okay. Is it a celebration?"

"And how." Connie smiled into the stained old mirror above the sink. "This thing makes a girl look forty, I swear." She preened, ignoring the frigid glances of two middle-aged women who were waiting to use the sink. "Celebration hardly begins to *describe* it." She wet a finger and smoothed her brows. "I quit my job."

"You *did?*" said Miranda in astonishment. She had never before met anyone who actually quit a job. Thinking about it was one thing, but—

"*I* won't be spending my life in this crummy building," Connie said, apparently to the air. "Let's go."

"Some *people*—" a voice said to their departing backs, and Connie giggled.

They got a small table in the tearoom, ordered the special, and Connie, leaning on her elbows, said, "Well, now . . . wanna hear?"

"Well, sure. But I certainly don't know how you had the nerve."

"Nerve?" said Connie. "What's nerve about it? People better themselves all the time. That isn't nerve. It's progress. And I am sure bettering myself." She broke off while their food was served, but was too excited to begin eating. "I practically got outa the habit of eating lunch at all. Been looking for something else on my lunch hours for ages. So yesterday this job came through, and this morning I quit. Oh, crimers, how I did quit. It was heaven. The look on the boss's face, I mean. They think you come with the desk, these men. Sometimes I think they don't even think you go home at night or have a life of your own at all, you just sit there holding a notebook in one hand and a pencil in the other till they get back. He found out different. Of course, I gotta give them their two weeks. But after that . . . *whoosh!* And I'll never come south of Grand Central again in my life."

"Two weeks? Won't it be awkward?"

"Awkward for who? Not for me, it won't be," Connie said comfortably. She ate a little of her chicken salad, put her fork down and said, "He even offered me a raise. 'Well, now,' he says, 'maybe I can see my way clear to upgrading your salary a little. You're worth it to me.' I felt like saying if I was worth it to him, why hadn't he seen his way clear to upgrading it a long time ago. But I didn't. Then he'd think it was the money I was worrying about, and it isn't, not really. This new job pays some better, but what I like about it is where it *is*. In a brand-new office building, made but en*tire*ly out of glass, up on Park, that has fountains in front of it . . . oh, my. They have so many windows in that place, it oughta be sunny at midnight." She went back to her salad, a satisfied smile on her pretty face.

Just like me, Miranda thought. It isn't the job that counts, but where you do it. I'll bet there are lots of girls like us who aren't ambitious but have to work, and of course it's where we do it that matters to us. She felt a sudden and unprecedented envy of Jenny, who loved her work. Jenny has purpose, she thought, but Connie and I, we're just marking time. Just waiting. Me, apparently, for Mr. Right, hoping he'll be just like Matthew Smith. And Connie—to choose, probably, from among her many Mr. Maybe-Rights. Secretly she thought that Connie had no more power of choice than a mirror had. She simply took what came before her. Probably someday, though, some man would decide for her, and that would be the end of Connie's job in the glass tower, and Connie wouldn't care at all. Meanwhile she was making things nicer for herself, so at least she had spirit. Why haven't I been looking for a job on my lunch hour? Miranda asked herself sadly, knowing the answer too well. She wasn't looking for something else because she didn't know how she'd face Mr. Pumfret and tell him she was quitting. A perfectly straightforward, cowardly answer. It was just as Barney said, she had no character. She couldn't do a thing that might entail unpleasantness. Two weeks of working around Mr. Pumfret after having made it clear she wished not to? Oh, no. It was unthinkable. Even the recollection of having refused John's self-assured request for another clandestine date didn't reassure her. Because, of course, if he asked her again this afternoon, when his father was safely away, she'd probably say yes. Barney was most certainly right.

Yet she couldn't help thinking—even if to no purpose —what it would be like to quit Pumfret & Son. She'd be delivered from John, from this street of buildings that looked, on this day of bright autumn sunlight, even shoddier than it did when the sky was clouded. From Mr. Pumfret and Mr. Camp and underwear, for the rest of her life. Another job, another office. Another life.

"What *is* the job?" she asked Connie.

"It's this firm of architects. They're West Coast architects, and this is their first office they're opening in the east. Say, Miranda . . . I guess there aren't any jobs left there, at least, I don't know . . . but why don't *you* look around for something else? You don't want to end your *days* in that hole. Except that neither of us would. We'll get married and all. But, meantime, wouldn't you rather work on Park Ave?"

"I don't know," Miranda evaded. "I guess I'm a creature of habit."

"At nineteen?" Connie shrieked. "Look, honey, you make a habit of that place, and in ten years you'll look like those bats in the washroom. I mean it. Act before it's *too late.*"

"Maybe," said Miranda. "Have you met any nice boys lately?" She picked up her fork and prepared to eat and listen.

When the lunch hour was over she returned to Pumfret & Son with her head spinning and her feet dragging. Another job, another life . . . And then she'd hear herself trying to say, "Excuse me, Mr. Pumfret, but I've just been offered—" No, she could not. He'd know darn well she hadn't been offered, she'd *sought*. And if he could make her feel the way he did over a typographical error now and then, what in the world would he do with *that* piece of effrontery?

Another job, another life . . .

John came in shortly, and said, "Say, what's the matter, Miranda? I mean, what's all this about tonight?"

"I just don't feel like going out, that's all."

"You sick?"

"No," she said, without thinking. "That is—"

"Then what's the reason?"

"John," she said curiously, "tell me, do I have to give a reason?"

"I think I'm entitled to one," he said stiffly. "If I ask you out, I'm certainly entitled to know why you refuse."

Is he? Miranda wondered. He sounds awfully sure. Maybe giving reasons isn't cowardly, it's just manners. She was not convinced. She was pretty sure Jenny wouldn't be forced to explain—

"I have these tickets for the *Pro Musica*," John was saying in a wounded voice. "I got them ages ago, to please you."

It'd please me more if you ever asked me first what I'd like to do, she thought, and said with a sigh, "What's the *Pro Musica?*"

"It's a concert of ancient instruments."

"That figures," Miranda muttered.

"What?"

"Nothing."

"Then it's settled? I'll meet you at the usual place."

"No! I mean, no, I have to go home first. You can . . . you can pick me up there," she said a bit defiantly. "After dinner."

After a moment's hesitation he agreed and, with a searching look at her face, suggested they'd better get back to work. "You're certainly acting peculiar, though," he said, going into the display room.

Miranda banged at her typewriter as if it were an instrument of destruction.

Her mother met her at the apartment. "Miranda, something's the matter with Jenny," she said shrilly.

"What do you mean, Mama?"

"She called up here a little while ago, crying like mad—"

"*Jenny?*"

"Uh-huh. Like mad. She says can you go over there as soon as you get home, and I said sure, so you better—"

"But what's wrong?"

"She didn't say. You better run along."

Covering the few blocks to Jenny's, Miranda almost did run. She found her heart beating uncomfortably fast, not from the pace, but from nervousness. She was afraid that something had happened to Jenny's mother, because she could think of nothing else that would make Jenny

cry. Jenny was not a crying type. When things went wrong
she became either angry or very quiet and firm. In the
years that they had known each other Miranda had never
seen her cry, and this was a rather frightening thing to
be running toward. Oh, golly, she thought, swerving
around a delivery boy, nearly colliding with a large
woman who yelled at her, I hope it isn't too awful. I hope
I can help. Miranda had always been sure that in an
emergency she'd go to pieces. She had never yet been
faced with a bad one, but the suspicion was there that
when trouble came she would not be ready and would not
meet it well.

Fearfully, reluctantly, she turned into Jenny's apartment building, rang for the elevator with a shaking
finger and rode up, taking deep breaths that she hoped
would calm her.

Jenny was at the door, her face flushed with weeping.
She pulled Miranda into her room, thrust a letter in her
hand and said hoarsely, "Read that, Miranda. I don't
know, it just seems to me that . . . Well, read it." She
turned away and stared out the window.

Miranda glanced at the signature of the letter and felt
an odd, angry relief that the emergency only involved
Brad. Why Jenny should weep for him, she didn't know,
but to go around scaring people to death— She looked at
her friend's nervous fingers running back and forth along
the window sill and felt ashamed.

"Fondly, Brad," the letter was signed. Fondly? She began at the beginning. It seemed that Brad was no longer

being faithful in Baltimore, Philadelphia or anywhere else on his itinerary. Brad was finished. With Jenny, that was. And he didn't think Jenny would mind. He didn't think Jenny had ever really loved him anyway. She was in love with her career, period, and he wished her well in it, but a man like Brad needed a girl who . . .

It was clear, though not explicit, that Brad had found a girl who . . .

She folded the letter, not knowing quite what to do with it, dropped it on the dresser top and said, "Jenny, do you feel awfully bad?"

Jenny turned from the window. "Yes," she said in a bleak tone. "I feel . . . cut down. It just doesn't make any sense to me."

It made sense to Miranda, but this didn't seem the moment for logic.

Sitting on the bed, Jenny groped for Kleenex, blew her nose and said, "It's like . . . something ending that you knew couldn't end. Sort of frightening. Do you see?" She stared dumbly at her hands. The flush receded from her cheeks, leaving her pale. "You're thinking it's just hurt pride, aren't you?"

Miranda hesitated. "Maybe . . . somewhat. It's just never seemed to me that you . . . oh, that you were enough in love to be this miserable, really. No matter what he did," she said frankly.

"Funny thing . . . people say pride is important, until it gets hurt. Then it's *just* hurt pride and isn't supposed to matter. I don't *know* if that's what it is, altogether. I know I hurt, horribly." She flopped back on her pillows as if exhausted. "And, I mean, he didn't even give me a clue. Letter every day, same as always, same *letter* as always, too. And now, as easy as that, he's in love with someone else. Brad!"

"He didn't say he was in love with someone else."

"Oh, Miranda. I suppose he still has some consideration for me. But I know Brad. No, no, I don't mean that. I guess I don't know him so well after all. But that's part of it, don't you see? Thinking you know somebody, that he'll be the way you know him, that nothing's going to change, and then all of a sudden you don't know him at all and *every*thing's changed."

Jenny and I, Miranda thought, are innocents where men are concerned. I'll bet Connie's had this happen to her a dozen times. Some fellow is around, and then he isn't. Of course, Brad had been more than around, he'd been wanting to marry Jenny. But that, too, had happened to plenty of girls. Someone proposes, and then decides maybe it isn't what he wants after all and sends a letter. But Jenny with her one man, and me with my none, we think such things can't be.

"Oh, I'll get over it," Jenny said. "It's just that . . . that right now I can't seem to look forward to anything at all. It's going to be so peculiar, without Brad and his letters and his visits. . . ." Her chin trembled and the big tears started to her eyes again.

"You can look forward to your job, can't you?" Miranda suggested. "You can't have lost interest in that."

There was a long silence. Then Jenny sat up and said, "That was the trouble, of course. It always has been." Her right thumb stole to her mouth and she nibbled at it gently.

"But you knew that."

"Yes. I expected him to come around."

"And he expected you to come around."

Silence. The clock ticked and the radiator knocked and a far-off siren sliced the air. Jenny took her thumb from her mouth, looked at her hands for a long time, put them in her lap and said, "I think I'll stop biting my nails."

"Can you?" said Miranda, surprised.

"I can try. After all, lots of things are changing. And I *am* getting older. More responsible, don't you think?"

"Yes, I do," Miranda said gravely.

"You've been a big help."

"I don't see how."

"Yes, you have. Just coming over and seeing me through this first storm. I'm better now. I wish him every happiness," she added grimly, caught the slight smile on Miranda's lips, and drew her brows together. "That's what I'm supposed to say, isn't it?"

"With a little practice, you may even mean it."

"Oh, well, I do mean it. Deep down. Way, *way* down. But, like other lovely thoughts, it'll surface, and then I'll write him a decent letter, and that'll be that. It's best really." She stopped, and went on slowly. "It's so darned peculiar, how you can *know* something, and believe it, and go right on believing just the opposite at the same time."

"I'm always thinking that."

"Are you?" Perched on the edge of the bed, her hair its old shining color, her eyes bright with falling tears, Jenny looked extremely pretty.

"Someone else will be proposing to you before the sun comes up," Miranda said suddenly, and they laughed, and didn't hear the apartment door open.

"A charming picture," said a voice at the door, and they jumped up.

"Aunty!" said Jenny. "When did you get here?"

"Just this minute," said Mrs. Long. "Let myself in with my key. Hello, Miranda dear. How are my girls?"

"Oh, fine," said Jenny. Miranda looked at her face quickly and saw nothing there but pleasure in Mrs. Long's arrival. With Jenny's fondness for her family and her passionate devotion to the job, Brad's memory was going to have a feeble time of it. And Jenny was not the kind to fan a dying memory, recalling his brown eyes and his laugh and the things he said. "Where fellas are concerned," Connie had said once, "there are two things a girl should have. Mad money and a good forgettery." Apparently Jenny and Connie, unlike in most ways, agreed on this.

Which, said Miranda to herself, is very sensible. I think I'll do likewise. And as she said it, she looked at Mrs. Long, who to her was an extension of Matthew Smith, and was filled with longing and remembering.

"What are you doing here?" Jenny was asking her aunt. "Mother didn't say you were coming."

"Well, dearie, I decided to come in and hear Mrs. Roosevelt—she *is* still speaking at the Club, isn't she? Your mother wrote a month ago and said—"

"Oh, yes," Jenny interrupted. "Mother will be delighted."

"And, at the same time, I have to get in touch with Matt. You remember Matthew Smith?" She looked innocently over at Miranda, who colored and nodded wordlessly. "Some friends of mine out at the lake want some moving done, and I thought I might as well throw a little business Matt's way, poor boy."

"Why poor boy?" said Jenny.

"Hmm? I don't know. I just said it. Because he works so hard, I suppose. And never has any fun."

"None?" said Jenny, tipping her head like a bird at an odd sound.

"Oh, I don't know, really. It just seems to me that he works day and night." Mrs. Long smiled, and looked around, and said, "Let's have some tea, shall we, girls?"

But Miranda had to go home for dinner and to get ready for her date with John. She went as though she were walking through sand up to her knees, and when she got home her father and mother were quarreling over Mr. Parrish's shoelaces. Or, Miranda gathered, over the fact that there weren't any and the ones he had on had popped past repair. It ended with his taking some from a pair of Barney's shoes and stamping off to the living room by himself. Miranda sighed and went into her room and looked absent-mindedly into her closet. After a few moments she shook her head, refocused her eyes, selected a dress and laid it on the bed.

And for what? she thought, half tearful now herself. I will get myself pretty now for John, who never notices what I look like as long as I listen. He will tell me how his mother hovers over him and spoils his finer relationships, how his sister is silly, how his father is autocratic. And I'll say, But, John, have you ever stopped to think— And he'll pretend to ponder, and then tell me where I'm wrong. He's always asking my opinion, and then, when I give it, justifying his own. Oh, it's all so silly.

"What was the matter with Jenny?" Mrs. Parrish asked when Miranda came into the dining room to set the table. "You going out?" Miranda nodded. "With him, I suppose?" Another nod. "Miranda, I hope you know what you're doing."

"Jenny's beau called off the wedding. That's what was wrong."

"He did?" Mrs. Parrish exclaimed. "Well, I never. She all broken up about it, poor child?"

"At first. She'll be all right."

"Sure she will," Mrs. Parrish said heartily. "The man hasn't been born yet that's worth giving a second thought to."

"Well, now, Mama, that's a little extreme, isn't it?"

Mrs. Parrish shrugged. "Where're you going tonight?"

"A concert."

"Well, there's nothing to complain about in a concert, but who you're going with is another matter. I just don't see what you see in him, boss's son or no boss's son."

"You know that has nothing to do with it."

"What has something to do with it is what I want to know. You don't even like him. You can't fool me."

"I . . . like him well enough. Anyway," she burst out, "I have to get out once in a while, don't I? At least he takes me to nice places. I call it a fair exchange. I get to see places I'd never see otherwise—"

"Oh, sure. He's such a heavy spender."

"I wouldn't get to concerts and things," Miranda said shortly, "if it weren't for . . . Oh, Mama, let's forget it, shall we? A girl wants to go out, and people aren't exactly lined up at the door waiting for me to give them a chance. What am I supposed to do? Stay in and look at television every night?"

"And you was always so particular," Mrs. Parrish said glumly. "I just don't understand."

"Well, there's lots of things I don't understand myself."

I don't understand why girls like Jenny and me don't have someone to love us. We're nice, and we aren't bad-looking, and I know that we're capable of giving love. Where are the men who would love us, and have our love in return? Jenny, she supposed, when she got over this first stunned feeling of being without Brad, would begin to look around. She'd probably do what she'd suggested Miranda do—go where the men were. Except, Miranda wondered obdurately, I can't think where that's going to be. She sees practically nothing but women on the job. Her classes? Were they really much of a source? Maybe they should both join the Navy. Jenny, though . . . Jenny might very well lose herself now in her career. She was so ambitious that it might be years before she got around to wondering about love again.

Could I, she wondered, learn to be ambitious? They said that what made a job interesting was what you brought to it yourself. Practically any job would have significance if you were interested in it. Practically being the key word. Because anybody with half an eye open could see that it was hopeless to try to make men's knit goods fascinating. Some work did not have within it even the germ of interest, and an open, inquiring attitude toward knit underwear would only make its dullness more apparent. *Mr. Pumfret, I find that I have to get a more stimulating job before I solidify with monotony.* . . . Well, why shouldn't she say it? If Connie could quit a job, so could she.

But the fact was she could not. If peace at any price was your motto, you paid even if the price was self-respect, and fun, and vitality, and adventure, and . . . You paid, apparently, if the price was everything except peace that made life valuable.

All through dinner and the drive to Carnegie Hall and the concert of ancient instruments she was fretfully absent-minded. She had arrived at what she felt was a crisis in her life, and to be obliged to respond to people rather than concentrate on what she must—and wanted—to face seemed an imposition scarcely to be borne. She was too little used to concentrating to be able to do it under these conditions. Even the concert—because the music was so queer and thin and pretty—didn't free her. She kept listening to it, kept being aware of John's way of half attending the orchestra and half studying her to be sure she was. *I want to think,* she said to herself desperately. I simply have to be alone to think.

During the intermission John explained to her that the rebec was the progenitor of the violin class. She stared into his face as if she were listening to the words of a madman, and said that she wanted to go home as soon as the concert was over.

"That's fine," John said. "After we have coffee." He moved on to the lute and the harpsichord.

They went to an Italian coffee house across the street, ordered Cappuccino and drank in a silence that only gradually made itself known to Miranda. She looked at him in surprise. It was all right for her to be quiet. She was trying to think. She wasn't thinking, but she was trying to. But why was John so wordless, so intensely and suddenly still? An uneasy, completely instinctive alarm began to rise within her, and to quell it, or make it meaningless, she blurted words that in her mind had scarcely form or meaning.

"John," she said, "I'm going to quit my job."

At the same time he said, "Miranda, I want you to marry me."

They stared into one another's eyes. He hadn't heard her words at all, and she was so appalled by his that the blood drained from her face and the dark room seemed somehow to tip and waver. This isn't fair, she thought childishly. He has no right to do this and make everything hard. And then, still rather dizzy and unable to speak, she said to herself, He's skipped a square. Do people ask you to marry them without saying first that they love you? The thought of John's telling her he loved her was unreasonable and not to be believed. It's unbelievable, she thought, because it isn't true. He doesn't love me.

Minutes passed, and John, for once, was subtle enough to hold his tongue. I'm going to have to say something, Miranda realized, afraid to speak. One word—it was going to be no—would bring down on her all the weight of his remorseless arguing and insisting, his plaintive, single-minded need. Marry him? she thought, and wondered why she hadn't known this would happen one day. John might not love her, but he wanted her with him, he needed her attention and her presence. He'd said, often enough, that she was the only person who'd ever listened to him. It wasn't a winning thing to tell a girl, but John wouldn't know that. He didn't sense things in other people, he only knew his needs and fought for them. She had a sickening prevision of how he would fight for this particular need even harder when she refused to oblige it, because that was his way. And John was clever. He knew whom he had to give way to and who could be bullied and persuaded.

Well, thought Miranda with an inward sigh, here's where I develop some character.

Chapter Thirteen

AT BREAKFAST, Barney said, "Would you like to know what it says on the top of this jelly jar here? It says, 'In answer to tens of thousands of requests, the growers are pleased to announce that there is now available at your grocer's an ECONOMY SIZE PACKAGE of this delicious product.' Now, what I have to say is it interests me to think of the tens of thousands of people all sitting down to write the growers, demanding this large economy-size package. Why do you suppose they do it?"

"You have to spend your time some way," Miranda said dully.

Barney looked up. "What's the matter with you?"

"What do you mean, what's the matter with me?"

"Something is." When she didn't answer, he said, "You look like an apprentice witch, frankly."

"Really? What does an apprentice witch look like?"

"Oh . . . wispy and wan. As if you were bleeding to death."

Miranda turned her head away. You'd have to understand Barney to know that this was concern, but she knew it. She was half tempted to tell him about last night. Barney was easy to talk to, and sometimes he responded in a way that was older than his years. The trouble was you never knew when the time would be. I'll have to tell them eventually, she thought. You couldn't keep a thing like a proposal of marriage to yourself. Especially when the result was going to be the loss of your job.

"I got proposed to last night," she said, thinking that her voice certainly sounded wan and wispy. No sleep, that was the trouble.

"In the words of Oliver Wendell Holmes," said Barney, frowning at the jelly jar, "who by?"

"I was hoping you wouldn't act your age this time. It isn't funny, and neither are you, and you know who by."

"Sorry. You shook me. I . . . uh . . . What did you say to him?"

"No, of course."

Barney let out a sigh of obvious relief. "It's not so of course, you know. I've always been afraid some guy you didn't want to marry would ask you and you wouldn't feel you had a right to stand in his way."

"Do you think I'm that much of a coward?"

"As a matter of fact . . . Well, maybe not. I just wasn't sure, you see. What happens now? I mean, it isn't going to be a very handy roomful, you and the old man and John."

Miranda didn't answer for a moment. She was thinking how different a man—or a boy—was from a girl. If she'd told this to Jenny, the question would have been, What

did you actually say? How did he take it? But Barney
accepted the refusal as accomplished and over with, and
he wanted to know where she went from there. Well, the
refusal *was* accomplished and over with, and she had
proved, for the first time in her life, she supposed, that
she was not quite at the mercy of everyone's moods and
wishes. Proving it had been desperate, awful, embarrassing, pitiful, and it was no wonder she looked like a
witch this morning. John had drained her completely,
and then all night she'd done no more than doze and
dream that it was happening over and over. Unable to
sleep, really sleep, she'd seen his eyes, his large sad face
hovering, wavering, approaching, receding. She'd heard
his voice all night. Sometimes it was imperious and sometimes pleading, but always it vibrated with the strength
that stubborn people have, so that she'd been repeatedly
afraid that if he kept on talking long enough she would
say, Yes, yes, I'll marry you. Because the sum of her
wishes and will would simply not be equal to the sum of
his. She'd awakened feeling destroyed.

"Now?" she said, her face white and sharp-looking, her
throat constricted. "Why, Barney, now I have to go down
there and quit my job." She laughed miserably. "How
much money do you have to be making before you can
resign a position instead of quitting a job?"

Barney's glance was compassionate. "Yeah. It's going
to be tough, all right."

"I don't even think I can do it. Could I call up and
quit by phone?"

"You'll want a reference, won't you? And besides . . ."

"I know. My character."

Barney reached over and put his big hand briefly on hers. "There is nothing wrong with your character today, Miranda. Nothing wrong at all."

"This is praise indeed," she said weakly, and laughed again. For him to tell her that was more comforting than words could say, but she thought he knew it. She stood up, feeling faint, wishing she could faint and not come to for several weeks. "Well," she said on a long shaky sigh. "I guess I'd better go."

Yet she lingered. Not entirely through her reluctance to get on with this day's business. She wanted to say something, and didn't know how Barney would take it. She wanted to say a word in John's behalf. He had proposed to her, and, no matter what, a man's proposal was a solemn thing. It was an honor. And in his way John had been nice to her, had showed her places and taught her things she might otherwise not have known. It was impossible to marry him, but to dismiss his proposal in the way they had . . . was that fair?

"No, but, Barney, don't you think he's—I mean, John is—sort of sad?" she finished limply.

"No think about it."

"That isn't what I mean. I mean . . . he had an awful childhood. His father's really a bully. And his mother is one of those women who think children are *possessions*, not people. Maybe if he were married to someone who respected him—"

"I wouldn't want you to be the one taking a chance on
it. Besides, I get sick of all this childhood jazz. It made me
what I am today, I better be analyzed. It seems to me that
at some point you assume responsibility for yourself. So
who had a beautiful childhood? It seems to me the time
comes when you better decide your parents did the best
they could, now you better do the best you can."

"I know. That's all right for people like you. You're
so sure of yourself. Maybe people like John can't do that."

"Then maybe he should be analyzed," Barney said
coolly.

Miranda fiddled with the strap of her purse. She was
finding it hard to swallow, and her stomach felt icy. She
wanted, she supposed, to worry about John, but she
couldn't. She was too desperately worried about herself.
"I suppose I'll have to give them two weeks' notice," she
said, and her eyes widened at the words. "Oh, Barney
. . . I *can't*. I just can't quit and then *be* there for two
weeks facing Mr. Pumfret. Maybe," she said, with a frail
attempt at humor, "John will quit, and then I . . . "
Her voice trailed away.

"My dear sister, there is no way out of this," Barney
said sympathetically. "You can't stay there. You know
. . . once it's all over, you're going to think this is the
kindest thing John ever did for you. I don't think you'd
ever have left that place if this hadn't happened."

Suddenly, as though till now she'd only been speculat-
ing on what would happen—if—Miranda realized that
this whole thing was true. That she had been maneuvered

—by John and John alone—into telling Mr. Pumfret that she was quitting. She had always known that she would one day, but one day and today were horribly not the same. Today was an inescapable reality and it had somehow to be got through, and then there would be the two weeks, and then maybe she wouldn't even *find* another job for ages. Her mind turned on John in a fury of resentment.

"This is all his fault," she said bitterly.

"Sure. I still say you'll thank him for it one day."

"Oh . . . I'd better go." She ran out of the apartment and down the stairs to the street and the subway and, as far as she could see, to her doom. It was just not possible for her to have Barney's far vision. After all, it wasn't Barney's problem *today,* and today was what she had to deal with.

The office was dark when she got there. Letting herself in with her key, she picked the mail from the floor, dropped it on her desk, turned on the light and looked around. Two more weeks and she would never do these things again, never draw a breath again in this room. I can hardly draw one now, she thought. It was peculiarly difficult to breathe evenly. Besides, she kept yawning nervously, and couldn't seem to stop. She hung up her coat in the closet, and looked at her alarming image in the mirror. There wasn't a mirror in the building that could make a person look anything but mottled. But this morning she probably *was* mottled.

Because she always did, because the work of the office

must certainly go forward, she sat at her desk and started on the mail. Slitting and sorting with cold, unsteady fingers, she stopped every time the elevator rattled up to her floor. Her heart, too, would seem to stop, and then slowly resume activity as footsteps went past or away from Pumfret & Son. It was like being offered a minute-by-minute reprieve from the guillotine, knowing all the time the blade must fall.

And then the elevator stopped, and this time the footsteps bore down on her and a shadow spread against the glass door. Mr. Pumfret came in.

"Good morning," he said, and strode on to his office.

Miranda closed her eyes and considered dying. Why, oh, why hadn't she just phoned in and quit? Was a reference worth this? But it isn't the reference, she thought, dragging her lids open. It's just that quitting a job by phone isn't done. And I don't do things that aren't done.

The buzzer rang. She lifted her head, drew a strangled breath and went in to Mr. Pumfret.

"Where are my son's letters?" he said. "The ones he dictated yesterday."

The state of her nerves was so bad that for a moment she didn't hear him.

"The letters, the letters, Miss Parrish. You've done them?"

"Yes. Yes, sir. They're ready."

"Well, bring them in here. Please." Mr. Pumfret's please was always a separate sentence, an afterthought. "I have to sign them. He's gone on a swing around our New

England territory." His voice as he said this was cross, and Miranda wondered sickly whether, for some unbelievable reason, John had *told* them. Forcing herself to look at him, she found Mr. Pumfret frowning at an invoice, clearly not interested in her at all. His crossness was just his usual morning crossness, distinguished from his afternoon crossness only by coming earlier. She went for the letters and stood leaning against her desk for a moment, wondering whether, since John had had the courage to be a coward, she could not also. Just let it go for a while. Say nothing. Then maybe later on . . .

She had a sudden stab of revulsion at the way her mind was going. To get out of doing something unpleasant, she'd sacrifice anything, would she? Well, she said to herself, ·I won't allow it. This time, this once, you're going through with something.

She burst into his office so quickly and breathlessly that he started back in his chair. "What's the matter?" he said loudly. "What do you jump in here like that for?"

"Mr. Pumfret," she said, and only knew she was talking because she heard her voice . . . she couldn't feel her lips moving at all. "Mr. Pumfret, I'm very sorry, but I have to leave."

"Leave? Leave, leave? What are you talking about?"

"About leaving. I mean, quitting. I mean, I . . . "

"You're telling me you're *quitting* your job?" he said angrily. "What for? You've been running around on my time looking for another?"

"No. No, sir. I don't have any other."

"Then why are you leaving? Give me your reasons," he snapped.

Somewhere in her mind Miranda formed the words, He can't talk to me like that, and suddenly she was calm. Not happy about it, and still nervous, but calm. "I'm sorry," she said again. "It's just that—" She stopped, because she didn't know what to say.

"I suppose," he asked acidly, "you'll do me the courtesy to stay until I can replace you? Or is that asking too much?"

Spitefulness in adults always surprised Miranda. Even in Mr. Pumfret it was surprising. But it did go a long way toward making her feel less guilty. At that, she thought, I've stayed here longer than anyone he's ever had. I wonder if Mr. Pumfret ever thinks about cause and effect. "Yes, Mr. Pumfret. Of course I'll stay." She hesitated. "Do you want to see the mail?"

"Of course I want to see the mail. *I'm* still running a business, you know."

"Yes, sir."

She went back to her desk, trying not to smile. Minutes ago she'd been in anguish, and now it was over. She'd told him. Her heart rose with the intensest pleasure she had ever felt in her life, and she stood, for a moment, spellbound. This was what it was like to face things. It wasn't falling into a pit of angry people who would frighten you and prove you wrong. It was crashing out of a tunnel into the light. It was being alive, and real, and sure of who you were. It was—she groped and groped, but could find no word except *heaven.*

"Miss *Parrish!* The mail. *If* you please."

Poor John, she thought. She hoped that one day he, too, would find he didn't have to be afraid of this man.

She rode home that evening strangely indifferent to the crush and the closeness of the subway. Swaying dreamily, she clutched her strap and planned for the evening. She'd have to see Jenny and tell her everything. She found that John was receding from her mind, leaving behind him just the fact of a proposal. One for Jenny, and one for me, she thought comfortably. Of course, this isn't *book*keeping, but still it's nice to be even. And then we can plan what sort of job I can look for, and where. Her light heart seemed to lift even further because of all the things there were to think of. And one of the things to think of was the fact of Matthew Smith, who wasn't a *type* at all, but was Matthew himself, and not so *completely* out of reach. After all, he knew Jenny's aunt, and she knew Jenny's aunt, and if a girl couldn't make a start from there, she was pretty hopeless, wasn't she? Matthew was a challenge any girl would want to take on. And Miranda was in the mood for challenges.

She got off at her stop and drifted up the stairs and walked along toward home with her eyes even further on the future than Barney's had been for her this morning. She walked right into the arms of a young policeman.

"Look where you're going, why doncha?" he growled, not unkindly.

Her face still alight with dreaming, Miranda lifted her eyes to his and began an ap logy that was never completed, because something wonderful happened. This slightly gruff public servant suddenly became, under her glance, an unmistakably private young man . . . biddable, available, for the moment entirely *hers*.

I'm *pretty*, she thought. There was no question of it. She could see in the snub-nosed, grey-eyed face of this young policeman that she was a pretty girl.

"I've only just begun to look where I'm going," she said, and smiled up at him, and, really, wanted to kiss him. "I haven't had much practice, you see."

He smiled down into her eyes and reluctantly, with a small sigh, stepped back. "That's fine," he said. "Keep it up." And then, as they parted, yelled after her, "Good luck."

Set in Baskerville
Format by Ernest Haim
Published by HARPER & BROTHERS, *New York*